Travellers
AND
Journeys

Paul C. Harrison F.I.P.G

authorHOUSE®

AuthorHouse™
1663 Liberty Drive
Bloomington, IN 47403
www.authorhouse.com
Phone: 1-800-839-8640

First published by AuthorHouse   5/18/2011

ISBN: 978-1-4567-7966-5 (sc)
ISBN: 978-1-4567-7968-9 (e)

Travellers's and journeys.

He had lived since birth in the same small converted boat house. Which in living memory had always been called Crushed Orchids. It lay alongside the canal and over the years the weight of the bricks and tiles had sunk into the foundations and it now bowed and lent into the waters edge, amongst the reeds and rushes growing there. On its canal side a wooden balcony which bowed forward and dipped with age with steps that disappeared into the canal. Along side that a thickly wooded landing, Its original use for unloading and loading barges in all weathers and conditions.

The Public foot path wavered near to his small garden that surrounds the boat house but apart from the occasional walker or fisherman was rarely used. It overlooked the canal one side and looked up to gently rising pasture strewn hills the other. On the opposite bank was where the horses pulled the barges along when needed.

As far as he could remember and before that to when he was too young to remember this is where he had lain. Not in this bed but in this room. It was the old loft room originally used to store feed and stores for the dark times or the lean times, when weather or unknown circumstances delayed celebrated arrivals.

All most all he had ever wanted was here in these five rooms apart from his mother and necessary food. His father was not even a memory, his name he had but that was all. His mother also now gone and departed. He lay thinking sweet dream like stories and mysterious tales relating to her nomadic family life as a water gypsy a bargee. She had told him every thing of her life that she felt able too up and to the time she had meet and ran off with his father.

Until that time she had lived in the old boat house. She had only known life in and around the family barge. She had been born in and had only ever lived on the same barge. Until at 16 years of age she had upped and ran off with James Rooney young Jims Father.

Polly Sparrowhawk. Petit, strong boned, jet black hair, and tanned skinned. A water gypsy, a nomad, with a family going far back into the realms of history and time. Coming from afar from distant lineage, wandering, searching, scattered races from the corners of the globe united in their search for survival and a place to find peace and acceptance. A strong and travelled race of independent minds and fortitude.

At the time of her leaving, or having gone missing the family had moved on. They simply had too, a barge full of coal to deliver and a barge full of leather goods to collect. It was not unknown for one reason or another for one of their kind to wander off or disappear for a while, not to say they were not concerned about young Polly who up tell then had never given them any reason at all to worry about. Other than to her coming of age. In all communities this is often a turning point in a girls life.

James Rooney (the senior)was by nature a solitary man. He had spent his days alone fishing along the canal. For many trips Polly had spied him. The tall strong young man with striking blond hair and engrossed as he was he could not help noticing young Polly. Who if could speak now would be honest enough to say that she had not only enjoyed but encouraged him to notice her. There courtship brief and passionate full of lust and desire that can only emanate from the young, if the two are of the same mind and at the same stage of being. At first it had carried on at night, in the folds of grass or reeds under the cover of the trees with the stars to light them, soon they took to the boat house and the comfort of the large bed within days they had decided that they were born for each other and Polly never returned home -she knew -he knew -she couldn't.

It was wonderful and thrilling. Hot and exciting. New and virginal-for both. On the point of boiling and both enwrapped around each other with the youthful endless energy and desire.

They did stop---to marry. In a small church which was in sight of the Canal. Nether sure of what denomination or interested. They did it because they both wanted it. Some where in both of them a memory of tradition. Two passing walkers were asked to witness the tiny ceremony and felt honoured and privileged to have been chosen. James And

Polly's union witnessed and blessed they soon returned to the Old Boat House.

The honey moon lasted six weeks, three weeks before the Marriage and three weeks after.-then Jim DIED. Some say from the intense passion. People say the strangest things sometimes they say the truth. Alone with her dead husband she was mortified. She hung on to his cold stiff body and if not been heard wailing by a resting walker a week latter she may of ended her days along with James in those sad and dark surroundings. Doctors first came then the police. They sent a nurse to sit beside her after the corpse was taken away. She was given morphine in ample amounts that freed up her brain and allowed her to soar above everything that was happening. Several days passed in this dream like state. the police returned with the news that she was free of any blame and that her Husband had died of Natural causes-and to try and accept the fact and not blame herself with the help of carers the nurse and morphine she dug deep into her youthful reserve and after three days was able to set foot outside the Old Boat House. Shortly after a man called to say that he had been instructed to organise the funeral. After the worst conversation in her short life it was agreed to have James Rooney's ashes put to the canal in a small ceremony of but one. After She laid his ashes on the water and watched them gradually absorbed into the murky waters of his watery grave. At this much latter times it sounds an odd thing to have done but at the time it felt as though it was the natural thing to do.

she had no idea.

She honestly did not know. She had no idea. Yes they stayed in the Old Boat House by the canal but she thought he rented it or just lodged there. She loved it because it was their home their love nest. It was not until the solicitors letter came. Which she took back to him unopened. James had shown her where his office was days after they had got married Telling her to go there if there was any funny business and he was not around. She had not known that the solicitor had sent it for she could not read, but she did know what a letter looked like and thought he would help her.

Before she had knocked upon the door it was opened for her. She was escorted into Mr Owens office and a seat drawn up for her to sit in. The young clerk asked if there was any thing at all she would like to drink. Thanking him but requesting nothing he lowered his head looked at Mr Owen and backed out of the room. Mr Owen was a very well respected Solicitor well educated and middle class but his appearance did not reflected his standing. He was in lay mans terms a hunch back with only one protruding eye to boot. James had warned Polly of this and she thought little of it.

Looking at her in her traditional clothing with her long black hair untamed hanging loosely around her shoulders and young bosom he could see the attraction for James Rooney. Her dark bright eyes long eye lashes and strong white teeth advertising her natural full red lips.

Almost pinching himself to stop staring he begun "EM Polly --Polly Rooney. Hello and welcome I am Richard Owen. Thank you for coming" With that Polly reached over and handed him the unopened envelope. For a moment he looked at it as surprised as Polly was when it arrived at The Boat House." Mrs Rooney I take it you have not read this"? She nodded acceptance."well alls well that ends well that's what I say -I had in fact asked you to come in to see me. First may I say how sorry we all are to hear of Mr Rooney's demise, he was a very important and loyal customer and colleague for so long." She nodded acceptance. To move on Mrs Rooney I don't know if you are aware of it or not but basically every thing that Mr James Rooney had or owned he has left to you.

Well every thing he had he has passed on to you.

His Properties including Crushed Orchids -his stocks and shares -his land holdings - -----.She Fainted.----- She honestly did not know--. She had no idea.-About his wealth---- or that she was PREGNANT! After much tender care and attention she was able to sit up and with a double measure of whisky to which she had asked for was for all sense and purpose concentrating on Mr Owen. "Mrs Rooney, Mr Rooney was an immensely wealthy man and would of wanted you to share his good fortune"---Adding to the effect how he believed that Mr Rooney would of liked the natural progression of Owen and Loosely handling his old affairs that they all knew so well. Mr Owen, not to be judged by his appearance he was in fact a shrewd business man and like James had been in stocks and shares with the help of James never in his league but much to thank him for from his advise and help he had watched James amass his wealth in admiration.

Mother and child

It was months no a year before she got the hang of having money and yes even longer having to use money. But what changed her life far more was the pregnancy and the arrival of young Jim. OH HOW her young heart ached -she looked down upon the lad as he had left her body, a small and tanned James. covered in the birth still but with his eyes looking up at her she felt as though James had been reborn.

Alone in the house without fuss or favour she had given birth to him her self some how completely naturally. Both birth and delivery. During the time pregnant she had brought baby things. For her in more ways than one a journey of discovery never having to needed to shop alone before or indeed be pregnant. Surrounded by cloths, stores of food and drink she and young Jim started out life together hibernating in the Old Boat House in those far off days almost oblivious to the rest of mankind.

As he grew their love grew months drifted dream like into years. Totally engrossed with each other their love and nature. Growing together in their river side home with the stars to light them at night whilst the water lapped them into a full and natural sleep. Still by day they avoided passing barges.

It transpires that James Rooney senior gone but not forgotten, had been the only child of an Irish travelling family who having settled down in Kent had been very successful by any bodies standards dealing in cars. Unfortunately it was in one of their prestigious cars that both his parents were killed out right in one of the early recorded automobile accidents on the then fast running A5 heading out of Dunstable near the Tilsworth turn heading for the horse fair at Banbury. At just 20 years of age he had been distraught and sort solitude and hibernation up and until he had meet Polly he had never had a relationship with any one else other than his parents before in his short life. All his hours were spent on his share dealing, he had inherited many but had the Irish luck and soon he grew to become one of the largest independent dealers.

Life almost in limbo hovering between ideal and a dream like state Polly and young Jim clung to and grew together as one, her no more than a child in her appearance they were often taken for brother and sister. As young Jim grew the striking difference other than the fact he was a boy was his blond hair he had inherited from his Father. In complete contrast to his Mother. It was in some ways though not completely one of the reasons that had first got them noticed.

Not troubled by to days laws and rules they lived an ideal life without money, work or health problems. Like his Father before him he became a dab hand with any type of fishing rod both off shore or with his beloved mother in their small row boat she had brought for them. He would catch fish both to eat and for the pleasure. A master of fly or float, proud to use his fathers Rod and tackle. Like all good anglers adapting and adding his own specialities. From a small boy he rode the canal in his small boat and come the summer learnt with his Mothers help to swim in the canal. Collecting duck and goose eggs from the reeds and the canal side nest when the opportunity arose. If none presented itself he would settle on drift wood and kindling to gather for the fire. If food could not be found or foraged they would stroll into town heading for the market and purchase any thing they needed -yes money was no object, but their needs were simple. They ate off the stalls on the market and brought some stores both enjoyed the atmosphere of the market and felt at home with the stall holders who seem to have something in common with them. Some of the stall holders were from similar back grounds and some thought that they might in some way be related to them.

She dressed more rural now than bargee her cloths exclusively brought from the market. Still she kept her hair long and natural it was still as black as jet, held back with a traditional head scarf. Young Jim would wear what ever given, removing all at night to swim in the canal. Often in only his woollen hat that he wore at all times both in bed and in the canal which doubled up as his bath.

Family ties

They still avoided passing barges. Keeping up the ritual of the past. She had left the family without word or warning. An unanswered mystery to all her family. This in itself was not completely unknown in their society, for one of them to vanish over night for no apparent reason often only known to them selves. Water Gypsies were not a non caring group far from it but had in fact developed not only a self protecting and fostering attitude to them selves but also to many strangers and loners who had stumbled into and amongst their fold. Many drifters and wondering lonely souls had reasons to be grateful to them.

It was by way of one of these such individuals that the Sparrowhawks got to hear of the tall blond young man and the petit young lady that had been spied in the now slightly dilapidated Old Boat House. Young Jim was only just sixteen but stood over six foot tall as had his father from his build and stature there's those that would have sworn that in fact that's who he was. Rumours and stories moved around the Canal communities like drifting snow or autumn leaves in the water no rhyme or reason they came and went as with natures seasons.

One such rumour had it that the tall blond man held the petit dark girl as in a power that she could not break from or fight. Others that she was never allowed out on her own only with him as a guard. True to say she was never seen alone for she was always accompanied by Young Jim but if any body looked hard enough they would see that the two of them Belonged together they almost moved as one.

In the months that followed the stories and tales of a tall young blond haired man stalking the canal banks had lingered and fostered into haunting tales of tell tale proportions He the internal traveller holding an innocent bargee girl against her wishes. sending fear and trepidation to all who seek pleasure or in deed had course to work the canal. Polly had in fact contacted Mr Owen their solicitor and

had arranged for young Jim to learn to read and write getting so involved in it she had often shut herself away reading the old books that were stowed away in the barge sometimes for 7or8 hours at a time Jim took it at a more leisurely pace both not so fascinated and naturally more capable in both reading and writing. But however ....

The image remained the same. Small dark and female. Tall blond and male. We now know that this image was a die cast for disaster but for Young Jim and Polly this was one of the things that was so rewarding specially for Polly.

That night......Jim lay in his bedroom the loft room where he had been born. Exhausted from a full's day rowing, fishing and swimming and reading until dark. Lost in peace and sleep assisted by his recent discovery of the joys of liquor. He slept the sleep of the total contentedness. And the half cut.

Below in her small room, for she had chosen to use the box room as her bedroom so as not to use the old bedroom of her oh so short but unforgettable marriage. From her tiny room a door opened on to the wooden balcony and threw the small residing window looked out onto the peaceful canal that she loved. Like young Jim she had had a full and pleasurable day and like him had had more than a few drinks to soothe her to sleep.

Like ships that come in the night

They had a dingy not the usual craft you would associate with Bargees it was made of rubber and could be stowed away easily on board any canal boat. Two dark skinned short of structure but not of muscle. swarthy faced Sparrowhawk males docked. They tied the small craft to the balustrade. Tommy the oldest brother and Nook the younger they need not to talk they knew what to do and had no fear. This was family this was their right. They were on a mission This they would do whatever the cost was to themselves ...tonight.

Like feathers or falling leafs their feet touched the weathered wooden stairs without a sound. Trained and tried in many a nights stealth, they climbed the steps until they reached the platform of the balcony. Tom held his hand to his brother both visible only by the light of a watery moon, he lent forward with his other arm and held to the small window pain. Almost immediately returning with a look and a nod that Nook knew to be that she was there. POLLY- no locks, no keys no noise, silent only the sound of water insects and a few cries of distant animal night life. The green wooden handle enclosed in his hand he squeezed trying both left and then right and slowly gradually he opened the small wooden door without a sound or a trace of guilt. He was on a mission. He was doing his duty he was rescuing his long lost sister and threw years of stealth and which now seemed like training for the reclaiming the family treasure POLLY.

Both moved into the small room without a word or sound. Tommy moved some how naturally to the right of the tiny bed that Polly lay in. Nook the other side, both overcome by her presents. With the aid of the reflected light from the moon and the canal stealth like they approached her small "cot "where she lay, draped in her night shirt covered over by only a traditional hand made patch work quilt. Her knees pulled up to her chest absolutely quite and unaware of their presence. She lay on her right hand side wrapped into a ball so much as a child. Tommy rolled her into the quilt and Nooky took one end and without a single word spoken they carried her corps like to the balcony. Nook stepped backwards down the wooden steps while Tommy held firmly onto the quilt where her head lay. He followed Nook down as if by radar. Nook stepping from the last step cautiously into the tiny dingy. Tommy followed effortlessly holding the blanked tight to his neck. He too stepped into dingy and lay the small bundle on the floor. Both now balanced on the edges of the tiny craft. Tommy reached over to one side and produced a small paddle which he used to cast them off and soon they seeped into the dark of the night and away from young Jim ....into the cover of night and mist.

A new day dawns

Young Jim awoke with the morning bird song. He lay still in his wooden bed. Aware that something was different in his self. He knew he had a mild hangover and he knew he had a youthful erection, but it was not them. Light filtered into the loft house his brain was of fish, water birds, snakes, pheasants swimming and fishing. Things that filled his days he knew it would not last forever but did not want it to ever end. He rose and descended the stairs to the kitchen come dinning room the heart of the Old Boat House and ferreted around to see what was available for breakfast. His sheltered life had excluded him from normal childhood and had aloud him to develop without the usual pressures of teen age hood. He was the size of a full grown man but as yet the character of a boy. Still obsessed with the youthful joy and secrets of nature yet unaware that his mind like his body was naturally changing to that of a mans. He had become aware of his new growths of body hair. his thoughts wandering to things not spoke about with his mother. Any female he spied he viewed with a watchful eye. He was aware that his now hair strewed penis had grown larger and at times pained him when erect. long and hard and yet up to this time unused. As at some point all young men will experience whilst burning to become a man.

Yes to him at this moment to breakfast was the most important thing to him in his life at this moment. After searching high and low he could find neither fruit or bread besides a fry up. Putting on the large brass kettle which he had filled to the brim to save his mother having to fill again that day. He strolled over to the door of his mothers room and knocked...then called...then knocked and entered. It was light from the small window and instantly he could see that her bed, her cot was empty the room felt empty. The door to the balcony was closed the room was empty. He opened the outer door no sight or sign of her to be seen. Yet he jumped back as if he had been attacked or was ducking from a assailant missile. He pulled the door too and made sure it was shut but almost silently, for his own reasons. He sat holdings his knees working something out, he rose and walked out of the small room back into the kitchen area to the stove he grabbed the now boiling kettle from the stove holding the awkward load by the wooden handle with both hands returned to his mothers box room and put the kettle to the floor. Slowly and gently he opened the small outside door by the green handle. Picking up the kettle with his free hand he stepped cautiously onto to the balcony. He removed the lid held it to the side of the kettle and stepped forward at the same time emptying the contents on to the Adder that lay on the balcony floor. "GOT

YOU ...you bastard"....He put the lid to the kettle the boiling water not only did its job it also flushed the adder sending it spinning into the canal he took a deep breath of satisfaction and leaned over the railings to watch it float lifelessly in the waters at some stage he knew it would be picked and eaten by birds, fish, insects, slugs and snails. The way of all things he thought. For one brief moment a rest bite from thoughts of his mother.

Going back home

Much before that and unknown to him and the rest of the world the small dingy with Polly and her brothers in had reached its destination. A sleek looking immaculately kept working barge. Black and brown paint work with gold lettering, moored several miles upstream from the Old Boat House. On board and patiently waiting were old Mr and Mrs Sparrowhawk. The below decks smelt of ruff cider, whisky, rum, cigarettes, cigars and **the boys** home grown pot. They had prepared for a celebration to welcome back into their fold their long lost fledgling. Tommy and Nook lifted the almost gift wrapped daughter into the Barge. Whilst both carrying her They both stood back as mother and father unwrapped their baby their only daughter. But totally unaware and unprepared Bet and Bert Sparrowhawk had unwrapped the corpse of their loved one now cold, and motionless upon the floor …..”WHAT HAVE YOU DONE…..KILLED HER …..WHAT HAVE YOU…. DONE”…………… Bet screamed and then Bert.

The adder had struck …..Polly was dead..dead on arrival ……. Unbeknown to them ….the brothers wept..the parents wept. Unbeknown to them a swelling could be seen on her back opposite to her heart. There was accusations, there were near deaths of every member of the small family. They drank they wept they drank, the brothers smoked pot and drank and wept..Then eventually when physically exhausted but more at peace with each other they jointly decided to lay the small body of their Polly to rest. Albeit for different reasons. Collectively because the sight of the corpse was unsettling. because the sight of poor Polly laying there was disturbing. Because if some one come along they may get the blame for they had decided that Jim had done it. Because they wanted to put their daughter some where Jim could never ever get at again even if she was dead. So in the tradition of their own making they wrapped Polly up with irons and heavy tools from the hold then bound her in strong rope. Tommy and Nook Once again placed her in the dingy and paddled for ten minutes to the nearest lock and both muttering traditional prayers carried her to and lowered her into the deep dark waters. Casting a watch full eye in the dead of night for any strange movements. Far into the night they had fought and drank tell they could no longer talk coherently until the strong neat alcohol and stronger marijuana fumes had consumed them. With the knowledge that her tiny body now lay on the canal floor out of sight but at least they know where she lay. Four completely inebriated Sparrowhawks collapsed in various stages of preparing for bed. Oblivious of each other totally paralytic collapsed in a shared drink and drugged fuelled coma. Mum and dad in the barge

The brothers cast out in the dingy. Wrapped around each other, oblivious of danger to them selves almost unconscious. Nook was awake first almost tipping into the waters and causing Tom to rouse his self both were struck by the sense of dread, then both aware of the noise and the smell their barge was visible down the canal it was consumed in fire. They panicked. what could they do, scarper, hide until things settled down. To lay low. This was part of their living nightmare. The brothers set off along the canal bank and before too many miles Tommy with the knowledge was able to start and drive off in a van parked up while the occupants were out poaching. They headed for Leighton Buzzard for they had a contact there who supplied them with marijuana they knew that they lived not far from the canal. The vague plane was to hide up tell they could take it all.

If young Jim had not have got up so early he would not have seen the slim line of black whimsy smoke that rolled like a large caterpillar along the canal and tumble onto the undulating countryside. He followed its progress as it was drawn upwards across the country side rising upwards twisting and turning from the level of the canal and gradually disappearing into the atmosphere forever to be travelling yet invisible to mankind. Until sight of it had vanished into the ether he stood some how spell bound by the sight, on the small balcony still holding the large brass kettle. Looking away from the now clear country side. He once more looked into the canal for any sight of the adder which by now had drifted away from canal side and was now invisible to him. He was in a dream like trance still wondering where his mother had gone.

It was the sound that caught his attention way off but rapidly getting nearer. He took the kettle back to the stove and hurried back to the balcony. Now he could hear sirens and the roar of powerful engines, and the flashing yellow lights every second getting closer. Almost in panic now with the cacophony of noise and lights getting forever closer and louder, from his view point he could see the light reflecting into the larger trees and country side, never having witnessed any thing like this before he felt both fear and excitement. And still watching the phenomenon pulled on the rest of his cloths and boots to find out what was happening. In some coincidental way connecting it to the disappearance of his mother.

Still as in a dream or a trance he ran the foot path towards the noise and flashing lights had congregated. He knew these paths like no other his age and attacked them like a spring deer just set loose. With in twenty minutes he had reached the spot. Heart racing he stood on one of the few canal side wood and Iron benches that had been put up with peoples names on for he knew not why. From this vantage point he could see much more, here a heavy mist lay over the waters clinging to the reeds and the bank dense and lank shielding the water from the sunlight. The smell he knew not what but it was acrid and seemed to enter into him threw his very skin. His eyes watered as if crying and the stench seeped up his nose stinging as if been stung. The bank on the other side was packed by a composition of men and machines. He could see a collections of boats on the canal some had machines on he had never seen before. A large vehicle had made its way across the country side leaving its destructive trail behind it. The noise was of shouting and calling, whistles blew. Loud speakers barked out commands. Lights flashed. bells rang and then for some reason Young Jim become aware of a man in uniform further down the bank but on his side of the canal. He had to Summon up the courage and approached him very slowly. He was not confident with people let alone a man in uniform but he needed to find out what was going on what was happening. Drawing in deep breaths he drew closer until he felt confident that the uniformed man could hear him above the noise. Cleared his throat and asked " sorry to bother you sir but could you tell me what is happening are you allowed" The Fireman turned and eyed young Jim. Looked back to the scene then pointed "Can you see barge ...or should I say where the barge was" young Jim shock his head more up and down than side ways which the fireman took for Yes. Well bloody thing blew up….exploded like ….gone nothing left, only bits here and there floating". That was that, with that the fireman moved further down the canal and Young Jim was left to ponder.

Sitting alone on the wood and Iron bench beside the canal he surveyed the scene. Little by little the crowd and machines dispersed. Many people took photos he knew not sure of what. Police men and officials came and went all day long. He sat in a stupor, in a trance watching the story unfold and totally unaware of the passing time. His Mother brought him to his senses from the day he had been born this was the longest he had been away from her side, she was calling him, she was telling him his time had come, his time to carry on the eternal journey that his father and her family had trod to journey on for theirs was a never ending journey.

He rose and made his way back to the Old Boat House. Hungry, cold and tired. Made his way to his unmade bed in the loft room and wrapped his self in his bed cloths pulling them tight around him much as his mother had done for when he was younger. The light had gone from the day he shut his eyes and slept dreamless alone and still.

The Sparrowhawks were no more they had crashed out in their barge, they lay to the floor inebriated, castrated, morbid and annihilated. Hating, weeping, stumbling, chocking. Oblivious to the time or traditions. Or even their trade. Bert Sparrowhawk had raised to his knees to vomit crashing his head he had in an unorthodox manner momentarily brought him back to a sense of reality. Temporally. He reached for and took the oil lamp almost by instinct in the dark of the cabin from its hook. Drew out his tender and lit the small wick, which was his last memory. Not a complicated story but with devastating results. The barge was loaded with vats of mentholated spirits every spare corner packed to the hilt. In the confusion and mayhem below deck, the usually most fastidious of men had been the instigator of the demise of the Sparrowhawks.

They say their souls still work the canal. Some say they still search for their long lost Daughter. Some say in the explosion that their brains would of fried and if they knew where she was before they would have forgotten now. In truth her body lay peaceful a further two miles down the canal in lock 77654.

When young Jim awoke that Thursday morning he knew that things had changed. Polly had talked to him of things passed and things if she should pass. That is how she approached things - in her words "One day when I am no longer here" or "when I am gone "and now she was. We all (well almost all) love our Mothers but because of his unusual upbringing young Jim was closer to his mother than lets say you are to yours and he had a indefinable nomadic affiliation and bond that only a single male child could have truly understand. The day of the Fire had stayed in his mind it seemed to represent a deep feeling of change in him be it that it was over a week ago he could as the young so easily do remember every moment **all though** experienced in a trance like state at the time. There's gone and there's gone he thought and she was gone of that he was certain.

She said don't forget for its not everything in life, but it is ours and when the time comes it is there. Which was her way of saying that she had made plans and provisions for when she no longer there. She had always said you know where I lay and that's where it will be ...but he didn't't know where she lay any more. It being what and he had never thought to ask.

Much latter that day only driven by hunger he rose did not bathe dressed in a fashion and went to the kitchen area in search of any scraps of food. Toasted stale bread heaped with on the turn liquefied butter and a hot mug of tea quenched his hunger for the moment. Feed and watered he felt revived. For no other reason than by habit he opened and entered his mothers tiny room. Like her he thought small dark and private. He opened the outside door to let more light in. Her small bed her cot as he always had called it lay still and empty of the old quilt that he had not noticed before the sides like a child's cot were raised within them lay her sheet and mattress with her pillow wedged to one corner. Without thinking he was drawn automatically to it. He could easily lift it or carry it. He was after all a powerful young man now. He bent down and moved it to the light from the window and outside door. Noticing for the first time that it was deeper than a normal bed and heavier than he had thought. It to him was now more of a memory no more an animated object but part of his history, his and his mothers history and now he thought his and his mothers past. Removing the last remnants of the sheets and the small pillow he smelt his mother he held them for how long he knew not. He held them to his self holding and drawing in the last living evidence of her being. Totally unaware of time. "ENOUGH" she said, he thought she said in fact he had said enough but it had sounded as if she had said…enough….He lowered the sheet and pillow carefully onto the balcony floor in readiness to lay them in the canal waters, no rules, no old tradition, just felt that that the canal was the place to lay them. The mothers cot lay bear, pine wood strips lay holding up the enormous (at least compared to the size of the cot) mattress not that it was particular interesting but he had never seen it before in this unmade state, never being allowed too make it. HE had made his own bed and yet if truth be known only in the last few years being trusted and having to do that task for his self.

Cashing in

He decided there and then in an instant to get the mattress out and put it to the waters with the sheet and pillow. Thinking as he did so what has happened to her quilt ...would some one steal a quilt, it was hand made and it was lovely but would some one steal a quilt. Once before a passing stranger had taken an ornament that sat by the door but why would you steal a quilt mentally engrossed on this issue he pulled and tugged at the wedged in lumpy mattress. Smelling his mother again on the heavy mattress he recalled the pillow and the sheet having realized that the task of putting the mattress to the waters was impractical. He held them away from his self and allowed them to float onto the water tears running down his redden checks. He returned to the bedroom and again yanked at the mattress. It was not tell he heard a rip and his left arm shot up from the mattress clutching a fair lump of its material that he fully concentrated on the task in hand. That was removing the trapped mattress from the cot. Young

Jim was not thick or slow in any way but at first he did not notice He did not notice that the entire mattress was stuffed with ....£20 pound notes ...., five feet five inch long, four feet wide, three feet deep ......full of £20 pound notes.

Polly never did understand stocks and shares, rents and dividends. the way she had come to terms with all that money left to her was to have, literally have it in money. Early in her new life she upped and sold and converted all of her husbands wealth into the only thing that she could understand hard cash. Every thing. Much to the concern of her solicitors Mr Richard Owen. Strong weald as her forefathers she had pursued the unusual request unabated. She told no man or women where and what she did with the large withdrawals of money. The mere logistics of it took her several months of signing..waiting....with drawing..and storing.

Here was the result of it £11,375,220 that what was left after sixteen years .....enough he thought.

He sat on the small bedroom floor with both doors shut totally covered and engulfed in £20 notes. In truth he never counted the money he could not ....he knew it was a fortune, too much for him to count. Just a blond mop of hair pocking out a huge pile of £20 pound notes. He did not relish the smell but he thought he would suffer it in his moment of glory. He did flirt with the notion that he would make a huge cash pile of it and set it a light in the small garden. A bonfire to his mother......it was a real thought but it was only for a moment. Eventually spell bound he rose, smelling of paper money, with tears falling from his eyes dropping onto the floor or at least onto the carpet of money. He had been there for many hours but never successfully being able to count all the money.

(not so surprising after all there were infact 568761 £20 notes, Young Jim would never have got his head round that.) All now of which he was gathering up to place back into the damaged mattress "bag". Core! When will me work ever end when will I be able to rest, Young Jimmy jokingly muttered to his self.......

Job done he stood in the tiny room feeling for the first time totally alone.

He took the remains of the tiny cot and carried it to the garden he placed it on his mothers favourite seat. when on any such night or during the day she would sit out and look along the canal route that ran virtually straight until it disappeared into the on coming country side. It rolled on to the wooden seat and lay at an obscure angel as if it were hanging on. He gathered the drift wood and bark that he had collected from the canal previously and lay it under and up against both chair and cot. he took a swan vester and lite the effigy watching the flames engulf an fold round the cot in the light of the fading fire and the streaming moonlight he returned to the Old Boat House.

It was a month may be more young Jim had survived, less than lived, Just survived. He had become haggard lost weight, unable or uninterested in eating. He drank, yes he drank too much of the alcohol that he had discovered. To be honest he smelt, unwashed, unclean if any body had approached him to tell him they would have not of got very close his mere breath offensive. He in that short period was retreating into oblivion.

Then one morning he had an experience an image of his mother standing there in front of him. Hands on hips feet firmly planted on the floor. Telling him off. "please take a look at yourself..your 17 not 7.......And so it was that young 17 year old Jim cleaned up his act. Jumping naked into the canal waters and not only cleaning his self but well and truly waking himself up. After soaking, cleaning brushing his teeth, and hair and nail cutting he dressed in his cleanest cloths he could find pulled on his new boots and rose a new man. Standing out side in the small garden for he had decided to tidy that up as well like his mum would have done. Having already tided up the rooms in the Old Boat House or at least to his youthful standards. Almost jumping he turned to see who had called out to him. It was infact a rather scruffy looking arty type. One of the new breed of canal dwellers, who found that life on the canal suited their way of life. Jim had seen them pass by watched them come and go but had never knew any that could be called a friend.

The man said" What is happening ....they gone and shut up the lock and say that no one can pass for three days "Jim stood staring not understanding. "they have shut up the lock maintenance or something. Do you know what is happening". He didn't't and he simply answered "NO". The stranger steered into the void and walked off. Young Jim carried on gardening when not so much finished but bored he down tools and it had come to him to maybe walk up to the said lock or at least the nearest lock to him and have a look to see this maintenance thing what ever that was.

He had blocked the few windows up recently in his depression. And when the foot path door was pulled too the Old Boat house looked abandoned and desolate. Clean washed and refreshed he walked powerfully along the canal foot path towards the nearest lock to him. All along the canal there was boats and bargees moored up more than usual and a good sign he was heading to the correct lock he thought. He looked ahead and downwards to ovoid having to acknowledge any body, or even having to say hello to any of the occupants. The lock now insight he was not surprised to see groups of men and machines. Parked and gathered around it. The lock gates were shut and a huge mobile machine was pumping out the water from the enclosed lock. Jim discovered that there was a damaged panel in one the huge gates that needed replacing. Feeling more human and amongst men that he need not say Hello to or acknowledge he infact felt relaxed. Dressed as he was he was taken for one of them.. Mainly fit young labouring stock. For an hour or so he stayed watching the waters gradually pumped dry reviling the now exposed lock. Whilst wandering over to the huge pumping machine to marvel at is exposed engine. He heard say that it was almost completely drained of water. He returned to the lock and took up a position near to the edge where he was not in the way. The floor was virtually dry of any water bar a few puddles and pools filled with black water. Towards the broken panel lower area of the huge lock gate pressed to the remnants of an once needed grill lay a small bundle. IT was his mother. Not incarnate, it was his mother. No one else knew yet what the small bump on the canal was but young Jim did. He stayed transfixed he watched as the ladder was dropped down to the canal basement and the builder climb down while two others held the ladder safe. He watched as he stepped of the ladder and reach down to the mound that had attracted all their attentions. He watched as the sodden quilt like a soggy skin came away in his hands. Exposing Irons and tooling and the perished bones wrapped in the rope when he saw the reminisce of her jet black hair, he turned away stepped from the engrossed crowd and begun to run towards the old Boat House along the foot path unnoticed by any one all others starring into the lock. when he got in he wedged the Door closed from inside. Climbed the few steps to the loft room threw his self upon the bed and wept his self into oblivion.

It was raining it had been raining for three days and three nights. The rain was blown across the open country side and rain clouds seemed to be relinquishing there load down onto the old Boat house. The cold box was empty of food. Tins once full were empty, jars scrapped clean and left on there side. Even the bread bin was barren. Jim had not been idol. He had scraped and shaved his emerging beard the evidence of cuts and scabs remained.

He had collected all that was important to him and it was packed in his haversack. He stored his fishing rode and tackle into the old loft room saying "goodbye" to it. With his best boots and newest cloths, now with the haversack on his back he closed the Old Boat House door he thought ---forever

WHAT DID HE DO WITH THE MONEY.............As I said he had not been idol in those 3 wet days and nights. It was secreted in a safe and dry place that he alone knew where. After seeing his mother laying in the lock he knew that when he put pillow and sheet to the canal that he then knew that in the canal is where she must lay.

He did have **£600,000** crammed into his pockets, haversack and underwear. So he was not destitute. Not yet any ways. He looked down the canal path where his mother had often looked sitting in the now burnt and unrecognisable old chair the opposite way to where the lock ran to where she now lay. Like her he could see and follow the canal until it disappeared into the open countryside. It was the way he chose to start the journey of the rest of his life. Young Jim became James Rooney and stepped out onto the path heading south unknown to him but onto the road to London and the home counties, he was leaving Northampton and canal life behind. That night and to his wonderment he slept, the sleep of the peaceful. He slept not alone but with an older woman. an arty type who had made her home on a barge along side the canal. Vera Reuters a tall slim independent and talented lady.

She was an artist who had a strong following of admirers both of her work and of her. Dutch by birth and proud of her heritage. She had not intended to bed Jim it had not even crossed her mind. When she had seen the young man stallion walking the tow path, she had wanted to paint him, his strong youthful figure ambling along engrossed in nature and aware of all things that were happening along the canal. At first he had avoided her presence and her barge, but she had set up her easel on the banks tow path and he had no option other than turning back or jumping in the canal of having to at least acknowledge her.

He had spied her long hair, high bosom and slender legs -but it was what was on the easel that struck him. The picture seem to cry out to him it resonated in his brain -it was the old boat house Crushed Orchids painted just as it was when he had earlier left it some five hours ago. Silent and all most hypnotized he stared for sitting in that old chair sat his mother looking down the canal. Stranger things have happened in his short life but the scene made him well up inside it was all painted so beautifully.

Her voice snapped him out of his trance. "Do you know it"?- Do you know it he thought, for some reason he was at first confused."Em-yes, I think I do -yes I do know it, it lays further back down the canal". "Vie yes -you do know it". Her Dutch accent intrigued him he had never heard it before. He replied "Why you have painted it in in spring -when it is often at its loveliest just breaking into leaf after the darkness " -"Yes your are right, I have more works below would you like to see them". He was physically tired having just walked for 5 hours and his mind was working over time he said "Yes". She upped her easel and paints and passed the painting to Jim. They stepped into the barge a traditional craft but painted in brighter colours than normal. Inside she had a sort of studio/ display area. Her paintings on display for all to see.

He stood in ore looking at her gallery, her pictures were hung around the crowded gallery, scenes that he knew and he recognised in her a joint feeling for the wild life and country that surrounded them. He wanted too but didn't't tell her of the fact that it was his and his mothers cottage in the painting. He asked her how much it would cost when finished when they agreed the price he asked her if she would keep it for him and promise never to sell it until he returned, she added that it would be finished in the next few days and was his. He paid her£250.from his haversack and with it back on his back rose to leave. Vera asked him where he was going to stay it was drawing darker and he had replied that he was not sure as yet. Offering him a glass of wine she said why don't you stop the night with her and she would try to finish the picture for him so that he could see the finished picture. Jim downed his haversack took hold of the wine and after a healthy mouthful agreed and felt more relaxed than he had felt in a long time.

After a little food and some more wine Vera put on some early blues music, whilst James washed and cleaned up. She lit candles that smelt of scent. James changed into his bed things. Vera gave him a drink of wine and slipped away to get ready for bed, returning smelling of oils and creams, she had changed into her bed things -much to James delight she wore a lacy top covered by a silk house coat that hung to her figure. Both seated in the only sofa in the room. She reached for a small draw and drew out two long cigarettes one for her and one for James, who looked on with bewilderment. She passed it to him and lit hers from the candle and then his for him. She drew the smoke deep into her lungs and he did the same before they had finished she rolled two more and James was introduced to the seedier side of life. Partly drunk and now affected by the weed he had smoked they talked of things not spoken of before and Vera gradually, slowly, gently Vera lead him to her bed and in the same fashion released not only of his pent up desires but also from his state of loneliness'. He felt more complete he felt he had become a man.

After a hearty breakfast of coffee porridge and toast both washed and dressed still sensing each other upon their bodies Vera asked James to pose for her, he agreed flatterd and then embarrassed when she asked him to remove his cloths. She said that he was born to be painted naked -and he was.

She sat him on a stool with an alarm clock placed upon his lap. He knew not why other than to hide his man hood, it was in fact an inspired gesture as she explained in all her paintings there was always a hidden message. This one was to say the Best of Times..He was a good model and would go into a trance like state enabling to relive the night just gone. After several hours Vera put her brush aside and said "Sorry James, so sorry God you have not moved a muscle how do you do it --I got carried away". James awoke as such still engrossed in thought " No its no problem for me I enjoy it "He still held the clock that hid his man hood, with his free hand he reached for his underpants and put them on. Vera smiled to herself at his shy behaviour. She made coffee and brought some malt loaf from the cupboard and buttered it for them both. As the sat he had to ask "Please may I see it " she returned with it still on the easel she turned it to him standing as it was. He starred at it wanting to touch it, he stood up and starred at it leaning forward with in a few inches he traced every line and shade of colour. It was him but it was beautiful, he could not believe that she had only taken a few hours to produce some thing so special. He felt proud and privileged to have this special relationship with this gifted lady not to mention the beautiful image of him self. She said he need not pose any longer and to get dressed whilst she put the finishing touches to the picture. Getting dressed he pondered I wonder what message she's put in the Crushed Orchids painting. Still with the thoughts of last night in his head his mind dwelt there and he greeted Vera now dressed with a knowing smile. This was her home and where she worked but she had a small cottage in Leighton Buzzard not far from the canal she gave him that address, she agreed to hold for him the painting of the Crushed Orchids and asked to keep the painting of him for her self" not for sale" she said. He blushing agreed. They hugged and kissed he picked up his haversack and only as a innocent youth could continued his wanderings, leaving the canal path heading south with a feeling that his life had only just begun.

Roads ahead

Jim wanted to leave the canal life behind unbeknown to him so did Nook and Tommy, Polly's brothers. Albeit for different reasons. Jim thought that the brothers were dead, having died in the barge fire. The brothers had no idea where Jim was but were still blaming him for the demise of their family. They headed off in different directions in search of different objectives entwined in the unfinished story of their overlapping lives.

Leighton Buzzard is a South Beds town laying North of Dunstable threw which The Grand Union Canal and the river Ouzel meander, surrounded by the remnants of the Chilterns. Some of the villages around it are remote and some properties are only assessable from the canal. It was to one of these that the Brothers were headed. They parked their stolen van in the car park of the Globe a river side pub come restaurant beside the canal on the out skirts of the Town, resisting the draw of a pint or two they headed for the near by canal and walked north bound along the tow path. Avoiding any Bargee people just in case they may have come across them in their wonderings and they may simply hold them up or even worse if things got complicated and things went wrong might remember seeing them. After a few minutes walk the barges became less, for they tended to gathered around the Globe -some for a drink some to fish and some to sell their craft wares a few to buy or sell marijuana. After a short walk they looked across the low lying field of rape where there lay The Stables. There was a huge black timbered building just beyond it the fir trees towered above it shielding the country side and what ever lay behind from view. It was to that and what ever lay there that they were headed.

Previously these stables had been only assessable by horse or foot even now this was the normal way to gain access, although now days the odd helicopter would be seen landing or taking off behind the trees. There was no roadway or even bridle path. The stables had originally been much smaller and used to house working horses of a gentle man farmer and land owner Mr Phil Costin. Who at one time owned most the land round these parts. Only to be too trusting to a bunch of travellers who moved in and established them selves in their traditional fashion soon to be of more trouble to him than it was worth to go threw the endless legal time consuming procedure to evict them.

From a completely different direction Jim also approached Leighton Buzzard but unplanned and unknown to him was on route to the Railway station by way of a lift from a young lady in a Range Rover and a horse box. It was a week or so after the brothers had found the stables. Julia was a country girl by way of her life style Horses, dogs, shooting, and Hunting. She from the start had gone out to trap James and for a brief moment she had. Jim still did not understand the attraction he held for females. When she had first seen him along the road she thought that he was a mirage. A mirage of the most beautiful Male figure a girl could only dream up. When she had stopped and he had asked for a lift, it was only then she knew he was for real, with out thought or normal concern for her safety she had asked him to put his haversack in the back seat and to join her in the front.

They were approaching the small village of Gayton a short distance from the canal. At first after starting up there was a silence James not wanting to appear to pushy-lacking conversational skills and Julia at first trying to come to terms with her predicament. Not very far along the road Julia asked "Where are you heading" Which for him was an awkward question, he answered. "where are you going" She smiled, her mind wandering. Wanting to say any where you are, but putting on a sensible head replied "Berk Hampstead eventually but got two stops on the way ". James did not think he just replied " That will do" She drove on effortlessly a confident driver and a happy soul. She explained that she had to drop one horse off and pick one up at Towcester and then drop that horse off at Stratford then head for home she did not think and he had no idea that it would end up taking five days, and that it would lead him onto a whole new world.

Rape Fields And Packing Cases

Mean while the brothers Nook and Tom were skirting round the field of rape respecting the rules of the country side or natural law as they looked upon it. The Sun cast a sheen of yellow on the ripe rape. Bent in pursuit of there objective their athletic figures approached the black timbered building stealth like naturally blending and moving into the country side. Without speaking they both crept along the side of the building looking out for any sign of movement. Both almost simultaneously lay to the floor on reaching the end of the Stable block. Movement could be heard but on tentatively observing their surrounds the only form of life around them apart from themselves was horses. Three horses and one small donkey. More relaxed now they took shelter in part of the huge stable in a sheltered spot and surveyed the now revealed area in front of the Stable block. What they had not realized was the reason they had got so far without being seen, besides without being grabbed or worse. It was that there had been an emergency and the look outs or guards as such were dealing with a less unfortunate intruder.

There were grapes growing in vines row upon row scattered between them were clumps of plastic covered low lying vegetation amounting to many thousands of them spread out before them leading to the woods it looked serene and idealistic. A peaceful country scene.(in fact the covered clumps were young marijuana plants) There was no house here no central concentration. It did not strike them there and then but the stable block must play a bigger part in the running of this concern than first appeared. After scouting around the area and eventually returning to the stables they having not seen any human beings but discovered more than enough evidence to know that they had indeed potted gold in every sense, decided to search out the stable. As they were about too they heard raised voices and shared laughter. Both apt at having to conceal themselves they both automatically went into hiding. There was a large wooden packing case away from the entrance against the wall without any discussion or prearranged plan Nook and Tom both went for it Tommy heaved upon it as Nook scrambled in holding up for Tommy to squeezed under as the packing case settled the voices and laughter arrived.

Lots of laughter lots of swearing and cursing and shouting. They could make out five people all men. Two with an Irish accent and three with affected English accents. The Irish were explaining that they had to get rid of the little bastard once and for all and the others agreed that they were right as long as they had disposed of the body in a place no one could find. To their amazement and to heighten the tension even more one of the English men said "Gather round this Packing case back here lads I have some thing you all should look at" They pushed and dragged the box a little away from the wall. With Nook and Tommy clinging to each other as never before. "That's fine lads now gather around this is the plan" The English man explained. They spoke for fifteen to twenty minutes about how they intended to expand the growth of marijuana distributing it locally and new inroads into Soho and the West End clubs and music venues and the open air musical festivals that were becoming more popular. The bothers cramped, encased and uncomfortable knew that they had arrived

Horse Dealing And Lady Moor

On the A43 heading for Towcester Julia and James were discovering their joint love for nature and as the time past amongst other things their joint love for each other. It was a youthful appreciation society. Both drawn to the others firm and lithe bodies. He had only ever been with Vera. The experience was to stay with him for ever but with a natural human erg to experience that beautiful memory with some one else. She on the other hand had lain with men before but James had more draw than any of the others had ever had. They stopped at a large farm house set way of the road and Julia Knocked soon a middle age Farmer and his teenage daughter came to the door and he directed Julia to the stables to the side, she parked the trailer and Range Rover near to the first stable and with the help of Jim lead the horse out, the daughter shutting the doors. Julia lead the horse out from the joining block and without a problem lead it into the trailer. After hand shakes a cup of tea, the handing over of some money and thank you they were on there way cutting back to Woodburcote to Watling Street heading for Stratford

They pulled up at a enormous Farm house and waited for the occupants. Julia explained to James that this was Lady Moors house an eccentric if ever there was one. James had this idea of a sweet old lady in large hats. What came to the door was a tall slim buxom lady of about forty with no hat or any other clothing. His eyes popped out of his head both Julia and Lady Moor roared with laughter at his predicament. He smiled and felt his face redden his mind all ready burning with desire before this display of femininity. She welcomed them in saying be seated while I slip into something. Julia explained to her that they would put the horse away first and James and her returned to the trailer. James very quiet, Julia laughingly asking "Did you like what you saw". James replied. "Nice enough-but id rather it have been you". Julia simply said "Thank you". They returned to the house and entered the open door A House Maid was laying out a small table with eats and drinks she welcomed them in and directed them to a huge sofa they sunk into the huge cushion drawn together involuntary but both pleased. The maid pushed a drinks trolley to them and offered them a selection, Julia ordered for both requesting large vodkas and lemonades. Lady Moors now dressed followed by another distinguished attractive similar aged lady behind her entered the room "OH Mrs Cooper bring in some cold bubbly dear", turning to Julia " Jules tell us about your young friend oh Jan would love to photograph him wouldn't you Jan" Janet a very good friend of Lady Moors had been engaged to photograph Lady Moors and in fact had been doing so when they had arrived the reasons she was naked, they had been talking obviously about this new male specimen.

They talked and drank Champagne, they talked and drank vodka. They discussed the horse and money exchanged hands. James was surrounded by beautiful women even Mrs Cooper the maid was attractive. Janet brought out her photographs of Lady Moor, it was very good he said(What he thought was nice tits and fanny) he was not an expert he knew that. It was after a lot of persuading by all the women once again he agreed to pose naked for a portrait. Music could be heard from the sitting room as he undressed and as directed laid on the floor resting on one elbow. The music got louder as the doors were flung open and Lady Moor and Julia came in with a glasses and a bottle of bubbly. They looked at him all three ladies light headed and slightly inebriated yes they were drooling, had he arrived in man heaven, well not far off.

In the morning when he awoke he lay with Julia he tried to remember what had happened and the memory made him think of Vera (you never forget the first time) but he knew he had to live for the day. One thing he did want to work out though was who had chosen the music and who was it. He was taken with the feel of it and it was not just the wonderful sexual experience the music kept playing in his head. He lay for long time not knowing what to do with Julia still asleep when from what seemed like nowhere Janet appeared wrapped in a towelling coat "Good morning James are you up for breakfast" and he was. He had not even thought of his nakedness not after last night but he pulled on his cloths while Janet woke Julia. As they ate a hearty fry up that Mrs Cooper had cooked for them. Whilst tucking into eggs bacon tomatoes and beans with rounds of toast, the others joined them and it was when they were all together with all the ladies vying for James attention that he made his mind up he knew he had a talent but what best way to use it

In the three days that followed James not only learnt about but meet some of the people who wrote, performed, recorded and arranged some of the up and coming new music. For Lady Moors friends were drawn from the bohemian society and she loved to be at the centre of modern culture. Although Jim loved this insight for him an unknown culture he instinctively knew that there was some thing missing or lacking in this protected environment. It was limited to a few privileged people. Perhaps it was a combination of his mothers and fathers family blood ties. His mothers family negotiating and moving various materials and goods along the canal and his fathers family although by rights travellers yet very successful selling cars and vans to the extent that they were the largest privately owned car dealers in the trade and his father in dealing in stokes and shares. Some how it was in his blood and he somehow more or less knew what he was going to do

Back at the stables the brothers.

Nook and Tommy were rather cramped inside the packing case, they had waited until the group of men had finished discussing what they intended to do about the distribution of the marijuana and all seemed to have left the stable. Gradually Nook eased the packing case up and with his head virtually to the floor peered out as best he could without realizing he forced Tommy against the side and the whole packing case rolled over both trying to dive for cover amongst the scattered hay however when the had both regained their composure realized that they were infact quite alone in the vast stable but for the few horses. The set up was far larger than they had imagined but being unable to comprehend what this might entail were not inhibited by it and only inspired them to get involved as they both thought in a big way. They knew quite not what to do. They needed to get involved but not sure who and how to start as night drew in it was decided to approach the first person or group of people and hope that they were recognised for they had dealt with Tony and Bruce two of the English men in the past hence heading for this destination armed with the information they had gathered under the packing case which they knew they could use much to their advantage they were eager and excited.

The evening was spent making plans and finding a safe place to sleep. Not that they slept much full of ideas and plans for the future. At daylight cold hungry and still hyped they looked for any signs of life other than that what nature was providing it was an hour or so when they heard the voices approaching there was two voices so they both thought if it comes to it as long as their not armed with guns what ever happens we stand a chance. As luck would have it, it was Tony and Peter. On seeing them Tony called out "What you lads doing on dry land" Peter looked astonished and said"Do you know these Tony"Tony replied. "Been customers of ours for a while haven't you lads"Nook was the quicker on his feet and replied"We are hoping to become a lot more than that" "Always pleased of a bit more trade, what you got in mind"answered Tony and then added "How did you find us without us finding you" Nooky made out he did not know what he had meant. He explained that in the past they had passed the stables and knew where they were. He then went on and told them of the Barge fire their ramblings and their desire to start something new albeit related to Canal life leaving out the overheard discussion heard under the packing box. This distraction however had the desired affect. Tony and Peter in return between them told Nook and Tommy about the set up at the Stables. A lot of it they knew from being under the packing case but they were able to put two and two together and with their hidden knowledge basically it was more or less as follows.

The big boss was called Danny -Danny O'Brian an Irish Traveller who had moved in and acquired the land from Mr Phil Costin-A gentleman farmer some 10 years ago. Danny's son Peter ran the day to day gathering and packing. The three English were all upper-class types who organised the distribution whilst Danny O'Brian collected all the monies. It was Peter who had caught the intruder and him and his Father who dealt with him and disposed of the body. The three English men Tony. Paul and Bruce left such undertakings to them to be honest would rather not even hear about such brutality but quite aware of its necessity, They often being out of the way distributing the goods. They had a team who collected and dried the goods but they were only temporary and came and went. The three English all meet at Stowe School and had first come across The Stables and its trade-in's initially threw fox hunting of all things and then their interest and dealings with the emerging music scene with its growth and use of drugs. Owning the venues and managing the groups and bands involved. Unfortunately thieving, blackmail and even murder was not unknown in the drugs trade and they left this more seedier side of things to the Rooney's. They were the front men to the business and between them things worked out and highly profitable to all involved.

However with the advent of the Brothers Nook and Tommy things were about to get even better "What we got in mind is expanding this enterprise threw our contacts and friends " Tony looked at Peter, Peter nodded then he said " Would you lads follow us down to the canal we don't build offices up here only attract attention, we got us a working barge as our office come and meet the team" And so it was 30 minutes latter to the sound of barking dogs they climbed aboard" High Times" a working barge. On board that day were all the team now joined with Tony and Peter. Paul, Bruce and Danny plus Nook and Tommy and an army of dogs.

Moving On From Lady Moors

Julia and Jim left Lady Moors with a fanfare they had been there for 3 days and nights Julia was behind schedule and Jim was on a mission. Julia was headed for home, she had to, late for every thing and not regretting a moment spent with Jim but knowing she had to move on. They had swapped addresses(Jim still owned Crushed Orchids) and had promised to meet when Jim had done what he had to do although neither quite knew exactly what that was. They eventually left, Julia with her horse money and Jim armed with Phone numbers and addresses of photographers, musicians, designers and much to Julia's hate models. After a short almost silent drive they pulled into Leighton Buzzard Station. Julia asked him if he was alright for the Train fare and he assured her that thank you that he was. Yes they snoged good bye and pulling his haversack from the back seat waving good bye Jim entered the station. Julia drove off as in a haze hardly able to believe what had happened and lonely. How could I miss him so much so soon -did it all happen. She knew that it had, she drove, she bit down on her lip and tears filled her eyes before too long she had to pull over and as never before she truly wept.

Jim did feel something but not in the same way as Julia and to his consternation he thoughts were in a whirl he had never been on a train to London before he wasn't sure where he was heading and yes he did already miss Julia. He brought a single for Euston he knew that was in London and London was where he was destined he waited on the platform having asked the ticket collector which one to wait on and every few minutes checking the ticket was still in his pocket. When the train pulled in there was not many people sitting in it or getting off it. It was Monday and 1.30 am most people were at work or about their business. Settled into a seat with his haversack on his lap not trusting to put it any where else. As the graffiti along the train lines increased he approached Euston as if in a dream soon to be rudely awaken when embarking and joining the maddening throng.

So many people, he knew not a soul, what do they all do, where are they all going he never thought there could be so many people in one area. He followed the exodus from the train and like every one else knew he was in Euston, for himself by way of the speakers announcing it. He produced his ticket he had checked for a dozen times and a ticket inspector took it from him still surrounded by the passengers he headed for the open air taking the stairs behind others he found he was at a taxi rank. he passed them by and walked tell he eventually came to the pavement area out side. He was standing in a small park transfixed by the endless traffic and the hum of London with its busy streets and huge buildings of offices and of architecture interest. He was as in a dream, then he was brought back to the moment by a young long haired youth handing him a flyer at the same time announcing that it was the best club up west. The Scene. Best club, best groups, best sounds ".Down Piccadilly way" the lad had replied when Jim had hurriedly asked him. Now he had to find where that was

Down on the canal.

The Stables barge was decked out like an office with a small area where there were 7 seats in a kitchen like area where all could sit and eat or drink whilst discussing things. When all had been seated and introduced and the dogs had settled. It was Tony who spoke first. "Now we are all aware of who is who. - I would ask Nook and Tommy to tell us of their intentions. Tommy rose to the occasion and to speak. "Me and my brother have been on the canal here all our lives and what one don't know the other one does. Our ma and Pa were both killed in a fire on the canal and we don't want to go back to barge work-our interest died with them-also we feel we can earn us and you a lot more money by way of our knowledge of the canals and of its various inhabitants. All sorts live on it and near it and the canals go all over and I bet we know most of them-those that do those that don't were you can where you cant. we could organise it spreading all over regular, honest we can". It wasn't a classic speech but within the hour the brothers were on board in more ways than one and they were making plans into the night. The brothers and the others testing some of the merchandise to inspire all. By mid day the next day the boys were loaded up with gear to distribute along the canal as well as an almost new launch that they could also sleep in. Terms agreed on a hand shake contact numbers exchanged and the brothers set of with Paul as part of the team. The brothers did not feel so at a loss and the Stable crew felt more assured of the new enterprise.

Within two weeks they had returned with a box full of money and an order for 5 times the amount that they had originally taken. That night after celebrating with the added company of two dark skinned strippers and a tape of some latest music, once again the three set out with more confidence from all concerned as to the out come. As well as selling what they had they had brought back contacts and forth coming events where a whole new range of customers would gather. This new life was looking good the thing was that Nook and Tommy needed to get rid of Paul, he was spoiling their plans for the future. They had all bonded and were mates but somewhere deep inside they knew that blood was thicker than water. They were both trying to think of a way of getting ride of Paul without having to kill him to be blunt. They needed him out of the way to instigate their plans. He was hindering them even now in the Launch. They couldn't talk or discuss plans only when he was out the way which was never for long. They had a plan to dispose of him but they needed to talk and fine tune their actions. They had food, drink, money and a few weapons beside the vast marijuana supplies. there fore it was difficult to enough to find space enough to talk privately. They headed towards their first customer which was London way down the canal a publican who had ample and willing customers for the weed. Nooky piloted the small launch while Paul and Tommy went below to get the goods ready wrapping the weed up in lots in Sainsbury bags to disguise it. First stop four bags, not bad they both agreed. When they had done. Tommy asked Paul to show him how to load the small Poachers rifle he explained that he had had not ever used one and if push come to shove it would be just as well to know how to load it and how to use it purely only ever in defence it had been agreed even before setting of on the first trip. Tommy's reasoning being as they were dealing in more goods and lots more money it would become more of a necessity to be able to at least be prepared for the worst, to use the rifle to scare off any such attempts, which made sense to Paul.

"Its called a poachers rifle because as you can see it folds over in half and can be easily hidden away" Paul was explaining to Tommy." They come in different cartridge sizes, this ones a 22 cartridge, you put them in hear then when you lock the gun back to it full length you release safety clip and not until then are you ready to fire." he then removed the cartridges put the safety on and broke the rifle so that it was locked together in half and handed it to Tommy. He held it as though it was a baby to his chest while holding the cartridges in one hand."Right come on its not very difficult just do as I did " Tommy put the cartridges down then locked the rifle into full length he went to release the safety and Paul stopped him "Not tell last thing" Tommy pulled a face and carried on putting the cartridges in holding the gun downwards all very awkwardly but concentrating he put his right hand over the trigger mechanism holding the short rifle with his arm looking for the safety with his left hand all very dithery. Paul could stand it no longer and leaning over and in an attempt to both help and take the rifle off him. Tommy in a movement as in passing it over all hands and fingers of both wrapped around the gun It went off both were thrown back cursing and screaming both at each other and in shock. Tommy was the first to rise the gun lay beside them Paul lay holding his gut, blood was pouring between his fingers staining his cloths. "Fuck my luck -not your fault Tommy "With that Tommy thought job done." Hold on me and me brother get you to Hospital".

They left him in Stoke Mandival Hospital. Paul told the staff that he had had an accident with his shot gun and that these lads had helped him to get there. He had complications and still the 22 carteridge in him and would be in for 3 to 4 weeks at least if he was lucky. The two brothers had fooled everyone being dab hands with the poacher gun since small lads. They celebrated down the road with rum and beer and headed back to the canal where the launch was.

Ban the bomb

Jim had to find Piccadilly Circus. He was not sure how far it was and without wanting to make out how naïve he was in London he was reluctant to hail a Taxi in case it was round the corner, besides he was beginning to get more confidence moving amongst the people. No one seem to notice him and gradually he was beginning to drink in the air and feel of London. After a while of aimless wanderings he saw a Policeman taking notes of a parked car, he decided to approach him and stood as it were at his feet waiting for him to finish writing. While he was looking at the ground the Policeman said "is this yours" "No - I just wanted to ask you the way" Jim replied. "Are you sure its not yours, if you are, ask away" relieved it was not his Jim replied."To Piccadilly Circus please." OH your one of them are you " Said the Policeman "What do you mean officer" The policeman smiled and said." A Ban the Bomber". Jim didn't't know what he was talking about but as he had smiled when he said it he just nodded in agreement.

The police man told him to behave and with directions sent him on his way.

Before he had got within sight of Piccadilly he could hear drums and chanting which as he got nearer got louder. The whole street road and pavement were full of people with banners and placards. A circle with a sort of rocket in which he soon learnt was the Ban the Bomb Sign. People chanting and waving there hands. Tommy was soon caught up in the throng. What with his haversack and long hair he looked quite the part. It was not tell later when they had sat on the grass and eaten drunk and smoked that Jim had listened in and had caught up with what the procession was really about. There had been speeches and demonstrations but the wonder of it all had been lost to Jim by the beauty of Susan a dancer she said at the moment in the London Paladium.After the demonstration they were going to The Scene a new club in the west end where the best bands played. She said he could get washed and changed at her place and added. "Its ok I look after you"

She had a flat above a cloths shop in Mitcham which she shared with a male friend not to worry she said hes gay." I hope that's not why you said you would look after me ".Jim joked " No your like him hes a character and a brilliant dancer too" Jim looked worried for a moment "No I don't mean your like him like that I mean, you know what I mean" Jim smiled. The flat looked onto the main road and was noisy and busy, but it was to be a place he would never forget. The Dancers name was David. He was tall and wiry. Very protective to Susan but not aloof. They asked David if he wanted to join them. He replied " Sorry darlings but I am working just down the road from you in the Haymarket, might join you latter though"Jim looked even better scrubbed up but Susan looked stunning -knock dead gorgeous said David. JIM just looked and counted his lucky stars. David who had dressed for work looked at Susan she nodded and he got out an Old Holborn tin and brought out three rolled cigarettes offering one to Jim."core my mum used to smoke that at Christmas time". "Did she dear boy what a girl !,but this is not Old Holborn its weed " Susan broke in with, " Don't worry Jim just try it, its better for you than you think a lot of our crowd use it" They all light up Jim following them by inhaling and holding it in t o maximise the effect. It was cool man and he felt chilled. Or so he said actually he felt a bit light headed and sick. When they had all ground out and got rid of the buts they locked up and headed for the railway station to head up west.

David departed down the Tube for work and they headed for the Shakespeare pub it was near The Palladium and at the of Carnaby street. The place to get the latest cloths she had said. The pub was well used by staff and stars of the palladium as well as westenders. It was always busy and full and often a famous face could be seen relaxing with fellow performers. As they walked in a buzz went up for it was full of Palladium Staff and Minor performers almost like family they were welcomed into the Palladium gatherings. Smoky almost hazy the music played and the crowd were introduced to Jim. Popular with the girls and the boys for the same reason all making up to him with the same intentions as one of the very attractive male dancers after all this is the 60s. Atfer an hour or so now eight of them decided to go onto The Scene. This club was the place to be at the moment. Noisily the walked threw the back Streets and Alleys of Soho when they reached the club they had to queue with others to be checked and assessed before being allowed in. It was Georgie Fame playing and he and his band was as good as ever playing Live and captivating the crowd. All the crowd loving it and no one not dancing lights down and smoky the atmosphere was electric. The evening went as in a dream and Jim allowed his self to swim in and consume the evening. It all ended too quick and they were in a taxi rushing to get the last train at night or was it the first of the mornings train to Mitcham. Back home and in Sues bedroom. David who had not appeared at the club but was at home in the flat left them alone to sleep away the daylight hours. It must have been about eleven o'clock when David jumped on the bed fortunately they were both half awake after having done it for the second time-they both screamed and sat up." Sorry to rudely awake you two but its time to get ready Sue"They stated rehearsals at One o'clock. Before they left David had lent Jim some swimming trunks and Sue had got him a towel. It was decided that Jim would go swimming while Sue and David rehearsed. Marshal Street baths are just around the corner from the Palladium they all said goodbye in Little Argyle street and Jim headed for the Baths arranging to meet the others in the entrance to the Palladium.

Baths and Showers.

Though in the west end it was more or less like most local swimming baths with cramped changing rooms and showers obviously built more or less underground it had an enclosed in private feel about the place like it was some ones secret pool in the middle of London. Jim found a cubical and undressed a few men wondering past him as he did so he paid little attention put his trunks on and stowed away his things having only brought a small amount of money and having no valuables as such to worry about. He walked to the deep end checked no one was diving off the diving board and dived in, it was refreshing and warmer than the canal and a sight more cleaner he thought but later he thought was it. He swam crawl, breast stroke. back stroke and the butterfly. did forty lengths, lay on his back kicking his feet until he reached the shallow end then climbed the four steeps out. He didn't't seem to be out of breath he just shock his self looked up at roof then walked to the changing rooms. When he got there it was a lot busier than when he had first arrived he waited to shower with others around the shower chatting and as he thought waiting to shower. Naked, soap in hand he walked a few steps to his cubicle thinking he was glad he come when he did because it was getting crowded. His cubicle looked across the passage way to other cubicles all now full as was the passage way and not unusual in a men's changing room full of men young men with a few older smart looking undressed men. As he dried his self at first he was not aware of it but nearer to drying himself he thought they were getting nearer or that there was more of them or both. He was virtually dry and just drying his private area when he realized they were all most touching him he looked up at maybe ten faces all peering at his private area."Do you mind " he shouted covering up his manhood whilst trying to pull on his pants."how much do you wont"one of them said "get out will you I am trying to get dressed what's going on"Jim replied "As if you don't know" a blond haired young man shouted. There was no doors on the cubicle and Jim was penned in. Almost naked and surrounded by aroused, healthy fit excited men. Jim felt vulnerable what was going on."Get out of his cubicle you perves"Boomed a Scottish accent before you could shout chase me Jim had the cubicle to his self. He dressed quickly and felt less vulnerable with his cloths on. On leaving the changing rooms he again heard the Glaswegian accent and saw the owner. He thought the owner would be like a bouncer or a body builder but it belonged to a smallish dark haired man."Some of the boys get a bit excited when they see a new lad Specially when hes built like you, but I could see you weren't't enjoying it" said the stranger. He wouldn't admit that he was gay and he wouldn't say he was not- Jim thanked him and asked him why he seemed to hold so much control in the baths. The stranger explained that he was infact to most of that lot their boss. In fact Jim found out latter that he was the boss to many more. He had come down virtually a penniless young man from Glasgow and had got into the garment game and then into retail and was rapidly expanding mainly in Carnaby Street. As Sue later explained hes the Man.

For what ever reason Jim and the stranger hit it off not in that way but in a bonding fashion. Jim told him that he had got to meet Sue and maybe David at the Palladium at half three. Steve the Glaswegian could not believe it."So do I"….what you know them."Well more David than Sue" he laughed. He had to get on and told him that he would meet them all at half three. And he did. David and Steve were in raptures at Steve's description of Jims Predicament in the changing rooms. Sue laughed as Jim did but in a compassionate fashion." Meals on me" said Steve and as they all crowded into Taxi."Ritz please, well get a bite there and have a gamble." said Steve and no one argued, within minutes they were being assisted out by the doorman and passing threw the beautiful heavy doors into the foyer. Where David and Steve signed Sue and Jim in. It was not until they were seated and were drinking their first glass of Champagne that Jim got to learn how Sue, David and Steve were all friends and how Jim had meet Steve."What a coincidence that you were both coming to meet us " claimed Sue and David."and it was they all agreed.

David and Sue went off to gamble, they were good friends what ever the situation. David was going to show Sue how you went about it and they all laughed at the various possibilities.

Over another glass of champagne Steve and Jim got to know each other more. Jim just said that luckily he was financially independent. Steve proudly told Jim about his latest shop and said that he wished at this moment that he had a bit more cash because he had the chance of an enormous corner shop that had just come up that he had always wanted, but that although he was not hard up he did not want to stretch his bank balance at the moment because he had also brought out right a beautiful flat that he just could not refuse in Jeremy Street. It was after their third glass and whilst they were having their fourth glass it was agreed that Jim would put in Half a million in cash for the new shop that they heard the scream.!!! It was Sue. Also drinking she had put all her chips on 27 not thinking that she was in fact gambling whilst having her one glass of champers whilst watching Jim and Steve making sure Jim was not bored and checking that he was enjoying his self. Sue had infact won £3600. They had to leave soon after to get the Two professional Dancers back to work. Sue stuffed the cash in her hand bag as she gave the taxi driver a 10 pound tip. She blew Jim and Steve a kiss and David and her disappeared into the back doors of the Palladium. The driver dropped Steve off in Carnaby street and then drove Jim back to Sues Flat having arranged with Jim to wait while he changed. It was well worth it for the taxi driver as he had already been well paid for his days work already.

Within an half an hour Jim appeared changed and carrying a large wicker bag."Going shopping" the taxi driver joked" No its some paper work for my mate" and it was full of paper. The taxi pulled up at Jeremy Street where Jim had agreed to meet Steve. He rang the bell but there was no answer.

So he sat cuddling the basket for safety in the corner of the entrance not knowing quite what to do and feeling a bit woozy and tiered after the Champagne. It seemed like minutes but it might have been as much as an hour that felt the prodding of a truncheon on his ribs."Get up from there we have had complaints your blocking the entrance" Jim still half asleep" that's all just waiting for --for um for someone"Now standing and under the wicker basket he looked quite reasonable, not the tramp he had been taken for. As luck would have it at the same moment a Taxi drew up and Steve got out, paying the driver off he hurried over and called out "What's going on Officer." It was not until they had taken the lift to his palatial flat that they had told each other what had happened. They had arranged to meet and Steve had got caught up in a documentary about his shops that he could not let pass and by the time Jim had shown Steve what he looked like crouched down that they had both roared with laughter at his plight. Steve made a cup of coffee and as they were drinking it Steve asked what it was."What is what "replied Jim "What is in that bleeding old basket" Said Steve "the money" mumbled Jim."The money-, you- serious " said Steve. Jim emptied out the basket and said " you ought to count it -I have"

trips up and down the canal

Their heads were soar and banging so to soften the pain from too much rum and beer the brothers decided to test some of the goods and both were tripping out and in a celebration haze to the launch of their enterprise. They more than any body else in what they had nicked named the Stable Crew knew the price that people would pay for their goods. They had worked it out they estimated that if they were allowed to sell the stuff on their own that they would be able to double the take minimum and so would be able to pocket at least half the money in the last trip they had grossed £2000 and that's how much they thought that they could of earned for their self's. So if this trip was to take 5 times that as was estimated then they should make £10000 for their self's. It was an opportunity not to be missed. Five grand each plus their cut from the Stable crew, for what, two weeks work.

Nook wondered if they got holiday pay Tommy laughed adding that it was one bloody great holiday from now on

They had yet to make their first drop on this trip so slowly and clumsily they lifted anchor and moorings fired up the engine and set off on a misty morning to their first drop at Hemel Hempstead to a group of travellers who were just getting into the weed. They brought it for their own use and to sell on as they travelled around. Some to their own, some to The travelling circus and some to joe public. Ither way they were a good customer and wanting more each time. They reached the locks near the Pub that they had arranged to meet them, on arriving there was no sign of them so the boys took the opportunity to fry up a breakfast and clean themselves up which helped them sober up and feel more human. It was as they were finishing their breakfast about eleven thirty that they spied the open top lorry loaded with scrap metal pull off the road and park up near to the canal. It was Wilf and Terry Frimley. Father and son team not to be messed around with or they would simply deck you and take what they had come for. They almost screwed the hands off the brothers and many a manly smack on the back in a macho friendly manner. They climbed aboard the small launch. Nook and Tommy had already decided to get the customer to agree on the price before any goods would be brought out. While Nook poured out four tumblers of whisky. Tommy was in discussion with Wilf as to the price and amount of goods required. Nook and Terry clanked glasses and both drank a good inch of malt whisky before lighting up a Benson and Hedger. As smoke filled the small room Nook was able to see Tommy and Wilf shaking hands and with a sense of relief picked up the two full glasses and gave them one each. Tommy nodded to Nook and he nipped to the locker and brought out a Tesco bag packed with the stuff. The Frimleys looked at it -sort of weighed it-smelt it and felt it. Rubbing his hands and looking at his son he said"Well deal done -but must have four times as much next time same price mind you, got a summer fair on and will easy sell it" with that he took out a brown paper bag filled with used notes, counted out £4000 on the table and watched Tommy count it. Four more whiskies and even more hand shakes and smacking of backs and the Frimleys were on their way. Nook and Tommys first deal and £1000 each better off.

Heading towards London way was a pleasure for the Brothers. In their new guise as launch people as apposed to barge people they could spy on all their old adversaries and colleagues, watching them at work and play and only exposing themselves when it was to their advantage. It was a busy part of the Canal system and they were for ever watchful both for potential contacts and everyday canal life. They had counted their profits three times and had now stashed it away. Both excited and at the same time frightened. Excited by how much they were earning and how much more they were going to get, yet at the same time frightened of what could go wrong. They both knew the score and it weighed up by far in their favour.

Berkhamsted was their next stop. It was here they were to meet up with there next and biggest customer. In the town away from the canal in the high street. The old town hall was converted into an up market shopping precinct, amongst which was a Café, where you could sit outside in all weathers.

It was there that they were headed. It was beginning to get dark by the time the brothers had scrubbed up a little, just enough not to attract any attention. It was only a stroll to the café just about long enough for the boys to regain their land legs as it were. They ordered two coffees and two pastries. Lit up two Bensons and waited. Both had two shopping bags packed- two with goods two without. You never could be too careful. By the time they were on their second Benson and starting to people watch they both saw them coming. For no good reason they both put a foot out under the table to check if the bags were still there, it was a knee jerk reaction because they could both see them.

"Hello lads sorry we are a bit late, want another cup"As Gordon sat down his side kick went into the café to order the drinks."while hes out the way lads I take it you got the stuff and as much as I wanted, don't mention how much or what it is ok"He smiled at the brothers as he lit up a small cigar. Nook was the quickest of the mark."you say don't mention the money -you have got it Gordon "Gordon drew out his coat pocket a brown envelope gave them a wink and said."Go in the bogs and count it, its all there." Tommy picked it up and within minutes returned with a nod and a smile first to Gordon then to Nooky. All four chatted about nothing and then arranged another meeting in a month. The brothers passed over the two bags with the weed in and all then departed the brothers to the Launch and Gordon and his unnamed side kick to his Lorry. Not just any lorry. An immaculate Lorry, one of Gordon's 200 lorries."He will be our best customer " Shouted Tommy when they were back on the boat counting the cash in front of Nook. £9500 in new 50 pound notes. That night they talked and planed for the future. They decide that they could make even more if they wer running things it was not going to be easy but even after this short spell of handling the weed and the cash they were sure they were up to it.

As they slept lost in thought and dreams, the stuff that they had handed over to Gordon was on its way around the country in various of his Lorries. Safe in the hands of his drivers. Some Gordon had grown up with. Some he was related too. Some he had spent a spell inside with. All he knew by name and about their family life. He looked after them and they looked after him. He had discussed this with the brothers and they were more than impressed.

A Corner shop opening

It was the opening of THE clothshop. Papers, Magazines. Radio and the Television were all there. It had been in the news for weeks. Music was playing not just music but new music. Live music from one of the most hottest bands around. The crowd out side blocked the road off from any traffic. 20 sales assistants and they could not cope. People jostled and danced at the same time. The four doorman hired for the day simply joined in there was no animosity. People just wanted to see inside the shop. to buy some of the new fashions. if they couldn't do that today they just wanted to be part of it. To see the famous faces, hear the latest music to wear some of the new fashions. Steve turned to Jim and shouted in his ear "Do you think its going to work"They were both pinned into the back of the shop and were reduced to serving. Their faces seemed to radiate and glow with the knowledge that could not be spoken in the noise and the hubbub of the moment. By the time the last person had left it was in the early hours. The shop was almost empty, Steve and Jim had only one thing that they both wanted to do. To go and get more stock for the morning. So in one of the delivery trucks they were headed for the warehouse. A regular driver at the wheel, just as well as the bosses were half stoned and half drunk but only as the young can do were able to operate being so hyped up and excited by their venture.

After Loading all the new stock and given instructions to the driver they were dropped of in Jeremy street to Stevens flat. Steve and Jim virtually fell out and the driver was soon on his way to Carnaby Street. Steve with Jims assistance opened the door not wanting to waken Steve's partner. They both stumbled up the stairs to be greeted by a not to happy Chappy."what am I interrupting your fun am I"Said Bill, Stevens partner."Bill you should have been there it was great it was better than I could of invented" replied Steve "And who is this Steve"grunted Bill."Oh sorry this is the guy I told you about Jim" replied Steve trying to catch his breath." In that case it's a privilege to meet you Jim" as Bill held out both a helping hand and a hand to shake. After a cup of coffee and a round or two of toast they decided that the best thing for Steve and Jim was some shut eye and made a joke about sleeping in separate beds while Bill was about which by the time that they had all chatted and bonded they could do with out any animosity or suspicious feelings from Bill. Suddenly Steve sobered up if that was possible."Bill where is he " Jim was startled. Steve was suddenly a different person, animate and eyes bulging, ready to take on the world."Like you I got carried away by the moment--sorry I would normally have told you as you come home--hes at the vets"Bill said as though he was going to burst out crying."At the vets oh my god not"----screamed Steve."No not that, I phoned him because I found a splinter in his back and they said to let them keep it for the night so that they could keep an eye on him knowing how much you worry"Replied Bill with now a much more relaxed face. Steve's body dropped as it relaxed as a tear rolled down his now smiling face."Sorry Jim my dogs been getting better I thought it had --well you know I thought the worse. Then Bill showed Jim to his room and went back to their room. Steve Shouted "Good night Jim". Jim shouted back "Good night Steve-- good night Bill"Bill shouted "Good night Jim". Then Steve shouted "Good night Prince" and as if rehearsed Jim and Bill both shouted together "Goog night Prince"

This lorries for turning.

When the brothers awoke in the launch. It was if they had been dreaming the same dream. thinking the same thoughts. As they got washed, shaved, done their ablutions, made breakfast the conversation was only of the idea of setting up with Gordon. The advantages, in away it was like a large family. Like a family they no longer had. No not the same but like it. They discussed like it had already happened. And in a way it had. Gordon's lorries not only went all over England, Scotland and Wales but to Ireland and even better Europe. Before they had finished breakfast they had made up their minds. They had to talk to him as soon as possible. Of course there was always the small matter of the Marijuana supplying but that could wait.

They brought a second hand Escort. Paid cash no questions asked. Tommy had the address and had phoned Gordon to tell them they were on the way. On the way to Hockcliffe on the A5 on the way to Milton Keynes. It was late morning and as they headed out of Dunstable nether of them had lost any enthusiasm for their new venture. Signs came up for Hockcliffe and Gordon's lorry company and as sure as they saw the large entrance a huge immaculate lorry with Gordon Transport in gold letters on the side was coming. After turning in they were directed by a series of signs to a visitor car park. Before they had both got out the car a burley boiler suited gentleman approached them."Hello gents, who is it your looking for"? "Gordon err Mr Gordon "Nook replied looking up at the mans chin, he was so tall he could not look him in the face."Follow me I show you to the office waiting room. It was like a decked out garage with a cold water machine and lots of magazines mainly about lorries. Around the wall were decorated with large framed photos of --yes --lorries, Gordon's lorries. Both got a plastic cup of cold water and were looking at pictures of lorries when a small chubby. suited but some how still scruffy man introduced his self as Derek then asked them if they would follow him to Mr Gordon's office. Sounding like they were the chosen ones. When Derek had left and Gordon had ordered coffee he then greeted them with a manly handshake. They began to relax a little. "Well lads come on tell me what brings you to hock cliff so soon since I last see you" Both did not know weather to jump in or wait for the other one to explain. Any how it was Derek who broke the silence."Coffees and biscuits" He placed them on the huge desk and almost crept out of the room. They were both thinking can a balding fat man in a scruffy suit be effeminate when Gordon brought them back to the moment "Come on lads what is it" Tommy reacted first Nook to engrossed in the Derek theory." Me and my Brother have been talking and after you left and thinking about what you said" Before the coffee had got could and before they had devoured the biscuits they had a deal. All on hand shakes and verbal agreements. Nothing in writing nothing recorded. Gordon buzzed his secretary his daughter Kate."If any one wants me tell them I be back in half an hour im going to show these two round the yard "The yard was huge perhaps 50 acres of workshops, Large store sheds, lorry and car parks. Spray shops, tyre stores. mechanics garages."Plenty of space for the odd bag of weed then"Tommy whispered to Nooky. After visiting the Lavatories and Locker rooms, they were on the way back to the Launch. It was afternoon time and the road traffic was quite light. What they had to do was to organise the growing end. It would not be easy but by the time they arrived back to the launch and found a good place to park the car, they had a plan the more they spoke about it the bigger it got.

Prince ---charming.

The morning had come and had gone. London rattled by out side but Jim lay in his bed fast to sleep and Steve lay in his vast large double bed with but a sheet covering him when suddenly he felt hot breath on his face and a very moist tongue round his ear he could fell the weight upon him and not being yet with it was conjuring up images in his head when he felt some thing hot quite hot round his loins at the same time taking in a strong odder that he knew and loved as his eyes opened he could see the face and fur of Prince a large white German Sheppard. Bill had been to the vet and brought him back, while making coffee for all, Prince had crept in and found his master. Steve only half awake still put his arms round as to cuddle Prince. Putting his hand into the hot spot which was loose dogs shit. The medication Prince had had affected his stomach. "Oh Prince--- fucking charming" yelled Steve. Bill arrived with coffee and whipped the sheet off telling Steve to wipe his hands on it also. Bill was laughing Steve was not. After showering and shaving. Steve dressed and headed for the new shop telling Bill to let Jim sleep until he wakes."You don't want Prince to wake him then " Bill joked. Jim did eventually awake and after a good shower and breakfast his head thumping still he actually felt a bit alienated. Here in this plush state of the art luxury pent house. with this bloody spoilt pampered white German Sheppard and this white pampered boy friend of Steve's he needed air and space.

He flagged a taxi and was soon pulling up out side the new shop. Still busy and to the sound of throbbing music. But know able to drive down Carnaby street unlike last night. It was late afternoon and Carnaby street was buzzing. Some one took his picture as he got out the Cab. It looked like a tourist, but he had to ask why. It was a tourist -a tourist who just hoped he was famous."that man he said that you were Mr John Stevens he saw you last night"Said the photographer." No I am not, but I was with him -sorry to disappoint. Said Jim."NO its ok you still famous"Jim knew he had to get away. Without a bye or leave he walked into and to the back small office room."Didn't't expect to see you " Steve greeted him. They were soon looking at print outs of taking with a sense of wonder from them both. The takings were far better than they had dared hope for --things were looking good.

That night as by way of a celebration Steve and Jim went to see David and sue amongst many others perform in the London Palladium. Tommy Cooper toped the bill but for Steve and Jim it was David and sue who stole the show. They meet as arranged at one of the side doors in Little Argyle street. And headed for the roaring 20s club that was mainly a Black club but at this time of night attracted a fair cross section of the London scene, who were interested in proper Blues and some of the newer black American music soon to dominate the other London Clubs. It was based in the Beak Street end of Carnaby Street and was a bit like queuing to get into lift. But once inside you entered a whole new world. Young Jimmy Hendricks was trying to eat his guitar, well that's what it at first looked like but buy the time they had got to there seats and table they were like the rest of the audience big fans. If you never see another guitarist again at least you know you have seen the best. That was the thoughts of them all as David voiced his felling during a change over of acts. but for Jim it was not so much Hendricks that had caught his eye so much as two flashy dressed long haired hippy types who were standing at the back, where as soon as one group or another had surrounded them and moved on another sided up to them. They were quite and at the back but Jim could not keep his eyes off them. It was almost pitch black other than the lights from the tiny stage. He asked Steve if he knew them."I see them about but I don't know them" Steve replied. There was some thing about them not there cloths or hair -just some thing he could not name. Some thing he could not put his finger on but something that was upsetting him. He knew he could not go over if he could see them they could see him. He knew who it was he felt it he did not want to admit it. His mums brothers.Family.Relatives.Uncles.

He could remember the weighted bundle in the drained lock (his Mother) and he knew that they had to have had something to do with it. No one else would bury their dead like that. Mum had told him all about her families customs. She explained that because she had married an outsider that they had disowned her. He had only ever seen her family briefly from afar and yet he knew who they were. They brought all of her memories back to him in that dark underground club. Her body in the canal-Crushed Orchids.-Vera -The painting-the money. The adder. The others were so engrossed in the Hendricks experience that they did not notice Jims preoccupation with the strangers and his thoughts.

They all left together it was 4.30. John Mayall with Hendricks had finished of the evening and the talk in the shared taxi was of nothing else. They arrived at Sues flat as it was decided that Jim would not be to happy if Steve brought David home. Jim was quiet and all inquired what up. But was excused as tiredness by Jim. Who made a point of saying what a great night it had been. It was Sue who inquired further when he was not up to doing it. Jim then excused his self by saying that he had eaten some thing --something wrong that had made him ill but did not want to make a fuss. And sue had brought it. Getting up and making him drink water. Which he did. He lay there tell she had fallen to sleep tell he dared to think about and plan what he was going to do. He could not forget his mum laying there. He could not forget Vera and he could not forget the Money. He made up his mind.

Ryde where you walk.
Lakes that you cant swim.

The brothers Nook and Tommy were back in there second hand escort heading for Portsmouth. They had both slept well but were almost hyper with excitement. They had spent the previous night in the roaring 20s club and were full of ideas. They had not even noticed Jim and his cronies. They were far more occupied with gathering information. For unbeknown to Jim they were not selling but more like buying. They had spent all there spare time around the London Scene finding out as much as they could about The Drug Scene in London. They had discovered and were heading for a contact in Yarmouth on the Isle of Wight that could enable them to fulfil all they needed from a direct source and cut out the Stables. They had thought of ways of taking the Stables over but it would be far easier to bypass them. So it was to Yarmouth they were headed.

The crossing was calm and uneventful, the small ferry packed with holiday makers and delivery vehicles. It was a mixed bag and the brothers were of no particular consequence. Like the others they took their positions in the queue to get off and were soon making their way to Yarmouth Yacht Hire. The Boss was drummer in a well known local band and one of life's original Hippies. His offices were in an idyllic situation near to the sea on a rise with a harbour leading to his many Yachts moored ready for hire. Parking was easy and with the sound of overhead gulls, sea breaking on the harbour wall and the thud of bumping boats they knocked upon his weathered door. It was opened by a stooping once was 6ft 7in man with tangled hair, wrinkled face but some how still young Ian Baldwin. The boss."Hello you must be Nook and Tommy come in and take a seat"They talked for hours, they seemed to have a lot in common. Water people, Ian Baldwin had put it down to. They discussed money and amounts. Collection and delivery. Goods were looked at and new stuff organised. By the time they had left both sides were excited, Ian Baldwin had a large and diverse family from his many romances 23 children and 6 exes with mortgages which he had never disowned so the extra revenue was always handy.

What the Sparrowhawks had to do was sort out the collection and to find out more about the new stuff on the market. Gordon was the answer to all these problems. Collection-distribution and the new stuff. Gordon's Transport any where any place.

They had taken some cash down and brought some goods back both to sell and show Gordon. Back in Hockcliffe in Gordon's office between them they had priced up the new stuff put it into lots and agreed a split of the profits and every one was happy. It was decided that they would stop dealing with the stables and they were all sworn to secrecy. The brothers were more than pleased with themselves. They had come a long way since they had left the canal life

Needs must

Jim was now in the outside world and the thought of all that money lay hidden back at Crushed Orchids plagued him there was over 10 million and he was the only one that knew where it lay his head almost spun with what he could achieve with it and this had been playing on his mind since he had invested in the corner shop. He had to go back and get it. The money was a big enough draw. but it was as if some thing bigger or stronger was drawing him back. Crushed Orchids was his Home and his life up until he had upped and left. The time had come he had to return and get the money to continue his plan, his life. He lay awake Sue watched him wondering if she had upset him or annoyed him in any way. After a period when they had both lain there awake it was Sue who broke the silence." What ever is it that is bothering you -don't take it out on me"Jim was mildly surprised not thinking that in some way Sue had understood. "ok your right -I need to disappear for a while but if you will allow me I will be back"It was Sues turn to be surprised. Sue got a light breakfast while Jim got ready. When they had eaten they said their goodbyes both for some reason expecting to meet up again soon.

Eventually at Euston and on a Train to Leighton Buzzard a round trip but as a changed man. What ever happens or has happened in his life he knew he had to make this journey alone. Back to Crushed Orchids. But before that he had to collect the painting from Vera's. He had her address in Leighton Buzzard and was repeating it to the Taxi driver, reading from the card. The Taxi drew up at a tiny cottage near the centre of the town near the old church cut of from the two and throw of the town partial by an ancient wall and over looking an old village green a sort of village within a town. Before he had reached the door it was opened not by Vera but some one like Vera but a lot older. Her whole body seemed to have been twisted into macabre distortion of an ancient Vera. Her hair matted and stuck to her head. With a visual effort she drew out the words."You must be Jim-Do come in"

He never knew how she knew and he did not like to ask."You be wanting the picture Vera said"Jim was impressed "Is Vera OK "he asked loudly thinking she was also deaf."Vera is well gone away to Holland for a while"He had to ask he her so he did "Are you related to Vera ". As she passed him the wrapped up picture she replied." We are sisters". For some reason he understood Vera less. He thanked her and started to walk to the town centre. It was a pleasant enough day and he found a park bench, he could not go any further without looking at the painting after all he had come a long way to collect it, Sitting on the bench he carefully undraped it wanting to ripe the paper off but thinking better to save it and reuse it. When it was completely unwrapped he put it on the park bench stood back and studied it. It was every bit as good as when he had first seen it. His mother sitting in the chair looking down the canal -tears welled up in his eyes, it wasn't tell he had wiped them and took a fresh look that he noticed one in the sky and another aloft in a tree two Sparrowhawks. Both in his estimation looking down upon his mother. More than ever he wanted Vera.

With not much money in his pockets he arrived within walking distant to Crushed Orchids. Clutching the picture and a bag full of candles, food and drink. It was late getting dark and a bit chilly. The cottage was boarded up and going into disrepair but as yet had not been broken into. There were three locks to the door to which Jim had the keys all were rusted and damaged but after what seemed a battle he managed to opened, having still to barge the door open four or five times. It stunk of death, dirt, damp and anything else horrid beginning with D. Once inside he set light to one of the large candles and pulled the door too. Time had stood still he could more than just imagine his mum being there. She was in every nook and cranny. He sat down, deep breaths and then a long swig of vodka. After a quarter of a bottle and some deep breathing he was back with the living. He knew he had to stay the night so he relieved himself went threw where all the knives and forks were kept and selected the larger items. He then ate a sandwich and drank more Vodka before he embarked on what he had come for.

Pulling back the carpet and putting it to a corner. He set light to two more large candles and placed them in a triangle.

The floor was made up of small tiles quarried from Totenhoe Knowls not so far away. With a large fork he started to remove the cement adhering them to each other it was a long and dusty job and after several hours Jim stopped for a drink of water. Under one of the tiles he wedged an old carving knife trying to dislodge it but it was too soon and he had to go back to working with the fork,. Heaving down on one with all his might he felt it move and so started the next stage of forcing the tiles up. By almost two in the morning he had all 8 up that he knew he had too by getting on for four he had scraped away enough concrete to see the steel cover. It was almost six when he had lifted the steel cover and by six thirty he was sitting covered in dust sweat, tears and money. After bagging all the money up into sacks, he covered his self up as best as he could and threw exhaustion simply made a rough bed of sorts and slept.

He slept but with livid dreams and recollections of his time spent in this cottage and upon the canal. His mother and rays of light and sunshine of the canal life and the nature around it and in it and of Vera that wonderful time spent with her even as he slept he was aroused by her memory and he could fill the touch of her skin and the warmth of her breath and he could smell her distinctive perfume fill the room and he could hear her she whispered" are you ok" in her Dutch accent and as he reached out he could feel her smell her and hold her because how or why he cared not she was there. She was there. Gradually he awoke from sleep, dreams became reality and although awake felt that he was imagining the situation. Vera held him close aware that it must have come as a bit of a shock to be awaken in this fashion but unaware of his dreams of her. They held each other for many minutes some times a kiss some times a tear. Together in mutual admiration."Why did you come"Jim clumsily asked."My boat it is out side moored up last night I hear this noise this your house I hope it is you and it is"replied Vera. Jim did not need to ask why she had moored outside he knew this was the only place that she had any chance of contacting him. He did not think this was odd he would of done the same."But your sister said you were in Holland" said Jim."My sister is my Mum and my mum thinks that when I am not at home I am in Holland, because I tell her that I can not have her on my boat she is how do you say it not right in the head and she would make my life impossible if I did not have my space to do my painting."I thought she looked old to be your sister" said Jim and they both laughed."What have you been doing Jim digging for gold"Asked Vera. The place and Jim were covered in dust and broken tiles, Besides two huge corn sacks filled with the money his painting wrapped the place looked like a building site even in the light of a few candles. Jim felt like saying better than gold I have been digging for cash. He obviously didn't't."Vera could we take these three parcels (pointing to the sacks and wrapped painting) to your boat and then we can catch up. Vera agreed and the two of them scampered aboard he boat with the three parcels. Vera set to making coffee and toast whilst Jim washed in her small bath. She lent him a bath towel and robe and took away his cloths to rinse out. Sitting in the small kitchen area they probed each other for things they wanted to know.

Her mother had lost it some ten years ago and Vera cared for her but at a distant. Her father had hung him self because of her mothers indiscretions, he was a weak man and could not handle it. Vera had never married but was happier that way. Jim showed her the painting and asked about the Sparrowhawks. She had lived for many years along this part of the canal and knew most working barges. Yes she had put them in the picture she said for many times she had passed or moored near Crushed Orchids she had witnessed one or other of the Sparrowhawks family watching or pointing to the Cottage. He then told her of what he had been up to including about Sue then he told her and showed her the money and told her about it. They ate breakfast. Vera asked if he thought Susan would mind. Jim smiled as Vera lead him to her bed. Jim undressed Vera and asked where to put the borrowed house coat he wore which by now was completely undone. Vera replied that she could see somewhere to hang it, when Jim replied where, she simply looked down on his youthful appendage. Discarding the house coat they fell laughing and excited on to the bed where what now seemed like a life time away they had first discovered each other and where James had lost his virginity and found his manhood. James had never forgotten that night and when some time latter they had lain together both breathing slowly and staring at the ceiling having both having accomplished total satisfaction. He knew why.

Double bubble

They were gathered in the long boat they used as an office. Tony Paul Bruce, Danny and Peter. Things had been going well but Paul had called them all together to tell them some news he had come across."You all know we have not got no rules as such but its agreed that we all look after each other-Nook and Tommy are not hear and its them its about. I got this friend a good mate who's got a lorry firm family firm fourth generation been in it for ever well any way they take on a new driver and he tells them his old company Gordon's transport earns a lot of money dealing in drugs and he don't like it. He says since the boss joins up with two lads from the canal they been doing it big time, I ask him who the lads were and he says he only knows them by the name of Nooky and Tommy!. None of the others could believe it. Bastards and double crossing Bastards was often used to describe them. Danny and Peter were obviously in charge of dealing with the situation. After much swearing and deliberation the group set out to deal with what ever had to be done. All agreeing that the brothers days were numbered.

Danny and Peter were not interested in why or how the Sparrowhawks had started dealing with some one else as well as them. They considered they had been double crossed after giving the lads a start in the business, in this trade there was only one penalty. Tony Paul and Bruce were left to run the Stables and Danny and Peter set out to track them down. They needed to track the Launch down so they started out in a small speed boat owned by the stables and began to seek them out. Out thinking them the boys had got rid of the launch weeks before so it was a long and fruitless search. By this time both parties were aware the other parties knew that war had been declared. It was decided that it was worth keeping watch on Gordon's Transport because at some time the boys were bound to have to go there and stuck for any better ideas they returned to the Stables and took one of the cars nothing to obvious for they did not want to be remembered or noticed a family Vauxhall that they used for errands for the stables. Having told Tony who was nearest what they were doing they set off to Hockcliffe. It was not difficult to find on the A5 four miles out of Dunstable. It was well sign posted. They slowed passing it and pulled into a siding. From were they sat they could see the large entrance and make out some of the interior. They could read signs for visitors car parking but noticed a large boiler suited gentleman standing at the entrance to it and were put off entering it. They decide to drive round a bit to check Gordon's Transports over.

Pulling out onto the A5 again they drove towards the light heading for The White Heart, pulling into the car park they turned around and headed back towards Gordon's Transport. Passing it they turned left towards Teddington and to there left you could see into the Yard. Lorries, sheds offices and car parks. But to the rear of it open farmland. Both nodded that was their way in. They drove back to The White Heart parked went into the Pub ordered lunch and a pint. Several pints latter they were walking passed the large entrance and turning to the rear of floor. The Transport. After 10 minutes or so they reached a small foot path that was situated to the rear of the yard. Both quite nimble and used to country walking they were soon out of sight and after climbing under the wire fence. Night was rapidly approaching but they decided to keep where they were until it was darker. So it was a few hours latter they approached the rear of the Visitors Car park which at night time was not light up. It was their intention to hide up in one of the offices or sheds and keep a watch out for the brothers or find some paperwork saying where they were based. It was at that moment one of the many office doors opened and they could not only hear but see the brothers.

"Thanks for that Gordon we will bring the rest Tuesday" they shook hands and got into their Jaguar car and were off. They knew what make they drove its number and that the brothers would be back Tuesday. Six days to plane their revenge. They waited until the jaguar had gone and the office door shut then continued to one of the empty offices with the lights out they were going to set up a place to watch out for Tuesday they intended to seek their revenge.

Double Dutch

Jim and Vera talked hours then made love for hours. They tried to catch up or even try to replace lost time. Yes Vera was older than Jim but not in her attitude or prowess. Vera was older but with so much more artistic talent. She was a special Lady and he an extraordinary young man. Together they could have every thing they both wanted. So it was with a plan that they headed for London in Vera's Barge. The day was misty and overcast but they hardly noticed both still captivated by each other and both counting their lucky stars, some how every thing had changed both felt it and knew it. The trip was slow they both enjoyed the animal life and nature along the canal and when not admiring each other they would point out birds and squirrels, fish, badger, fox and deer sightings.

The plan was to buy a building or an established Gallery in the Mayfair area and to sell Vera's paintings and other established artist that Vera was associated with. Jim would buy the Premise and get a commission on every painting sold and with his contacts in the West End and Soho they were confident that it would go well. As they pulled into Leighton Buzzard to moor up for the night near the Globe where so many barges gather. Jims mind was deflected into the recent past. Crushed Orchids had awakened in him memories of his past and now even with Vera with it clawed at his heart. They had chosen Leighton Buzzard to stop over for several reasons. One to see Vera's mum and to collect some paintings from her cottage. Also to drop off and collect some money from a commission she had painted. Although the money did not seem so important now. Vera had persuaded Jim to Bank most of the money. It was simply to risky to carry it about. She knew the manager of Barclays in the High Street and trusted him. They were going to bank 1 million and tell him it was from the sale of his parents house then to avoid suspicion they would put the rest in a safety box carefully hidden in a locked steel casket of her fathers.

They both approached Vera cottage armed with the camouflaged feed sacks full of money and a large bunch of flowers for Doris. Vera's mum. Jim did not know what to expect. Doris came to the door in exactly the same cloths that Jim had last seen her."Oh you decided to come back then "Ignoring Vera, Doris addressed Jim. He took the imitative and handed her the flowers."Yes and we have brought you these. For a moment or two she was dumb struck her distorted body took on a life of its own and her face twitched she looked like if there was one she would break out into a St.Vituss dance.. Vera took her hand and lead her in. whilst taking to her."Doris we come to collect a few things and to see if you need any thing. Jim drew up the rear closing the door as this was his second visit he was not too surprised, He confessed to Vera latter that he first time he was shocked by what he had seen there.

Vera poured her mother Vodka and searched until she found her supply of Hash. She rolled two joints, looked across to Jim and said."I remember last time you did not enjoy " She lite both and handed one to Doris, who after inhaling and virtually drawing in the whole lightly made joint seemed to expand, on breathing out Doris said " Does he know"Vera replied " Not every thing but we can trust him he is a special friend "Doris twitched a little then finished off the joint. She looked at Vera then Jim then back to Vera."Tell him while I make us all coffee " With that she stopped twitching and headed for the small Kitchen. Vera told him, Doris was her mum, she had a drink and drugs problem,---she had escaped from prison in Holland seven years ago for various drug related crimes and petty theft. Vera had hid Doris for so long she had forgotten what she was like before she had become addicted. This was Doris and Vera accepted her as she now was because in spite of every thing she was still her mother. When her father hung himself he had sentenced Doris to a life of guilt and regret.

Up in the spare bedrooms there was no room for anything other than Vera's paintings not framed but mounted on ply wood only two paintings were mounted one bound up in brown paper and the other one of naked Jim as a younger man holding a clock. They were carefully loading them up into lots. When Jim picked the framed one of him up Vera said "We can put it on show but it is never for sale"Jim replied

"I hoped you say that Vera " And they were both happy. Vera said the bound up one is a commission that we must deliver hes a good regular customer every time he gets a new lorry he ask me to do a painting of it not my normal work but a good customer, Gordon's of Hockcliff.

They decided to hire a van and take all the paintings to Vera's boat. That done to drop the Lorry painting of to Gordon's. They phoned to arrange this and as ever Gordon wanted to meet Vera not only to collect his picture but he had another commission. Vera said "Best day for him is Tuesday so I just said ok, we can wait here tell Tuesday or go back to the boat "Jim had to think fast he did not wont to stay with Doris but he did not want to upset Vera."Lets get the banking done first then we can sort out what's best to do latter". That agreed they both set to sorting the money out. Alone in the upstairs bedroom they counted out a million pounds they were to put in an account, then changed their minds and made it half that. This would still cause an eruption but not so much if it was a million. Jim took twenty five thousand out for ready cash. The rest they wedged into Vera's fathers old steel casket, which was large and heavy but only just big enough to hold all the cash. Having checked every thing over they carried the casket down to the hall near the front door and called Doris. While Jim spoke to Doris, Vera phoned for a taxi. While they waited Jim gave Doris two hundred pounds basically for drink and drugs but that was her affair. Saying that they would be back latter to collect the paintings. The taxi arrived they loaded the casket in and headed for Barclays. The taxi dropped them off out side in the busy market street. They did not have to wait long and were soon sitting with Mr

Lindsey the bank manager. He accepted Jims story and opened an account for him. Jim said that the casket contained Family photos and letters. And that it was important that it was safe. Mr Lindsey assured him that it would be saying."It would be safe even if it was filled with money"They looked shocked and then laughed. That done they went for a coffee to plan the next few days until Tuesday

They decided to get a hired van load the boat up with the paintings and then take Doris out for lunch. If they hired the van for a few days they could drive over to Gordon's in it. They drank their coffee and walked to the industrial estate where they hired a transit van. After picking up all the paintings and Doris they drove to the Globe where they had moored up and to treat Doris to dinner and no doubt a few drinks. Doris had scrubbed up well and looked more with it. She did not have a main meal only a starter and sweet plus several bottles of wine. She fell to sleep in the barge whilst they unloaded the paintings, Jim physically picked her up and carried her to the van. Vera climbed in and they drove her back to the cottage the decision having been made they would stay in Vera's boat tell Tuesday. They put her to bed and drove back to the boat stopping for a quick one in the Globe on their own.

c U Next Tuesday.

Vera and Jim spent the next few days planning their Art gallery. So engrossed that they hardly left time for eating drinking or even love making. Before they realized it it was Tuesday morning. After a hurried breakfast they scrubbed up put the painting into the Van and headed out towards Hockcliffe. Little did they realize that almost the identical time the Sparrowhawk brothers were getting into their Jaguar and heading for the same destination.

Danny and Peter were holed up in part of a warehouse in the rear of Gordon's Transport yard that over looked the visitors car park. They had crept into the previous night having discovered it when they had first broke into it several days ago. It was only 8am, but the boys wanted to be sure not to miss this opportunity to get even with the brothers. They knew the make model colour and number plate of the jaguar. They would sit and wait their chance.

The Sparrowhawk brothers were in good spirits things had been going well. They had a boot full of weed and boxes full of cocaine. Their link up with Gordon had far exceeded their hopes. Ian Baldwin their supplier in the Yarmouth was more than happy with them. Driving to Gordon's the talk was of expanding further and taking on people to help them. What to do with their money and where to keep it. The talk of success.

Jim and Vera now half organised were driving out of Leighton Buzzard along county Lanes towards Hockcliffe."How much do you charge for the painting Vera".Jim asked as they took a rather sharp bend near Egington."Well as he is a regular I charge him £500 "Vera replied." Bloody hell that's good money. Jim was surprised but pleased, thinking of his investment." It is, but I am worth it "Vera replied with a smile. They drove on until they reached the cross road and slowed at the junction with the A5. They stopped at the red lights and Vera Said "Now turn right in less than a half mile your see signs for Teddington its just before that on the left hand side..

Danny and Peter were getting excited. They were armed with various weapons and had a rough idea what punishment they would inflict upon Nook and Tommy. Their car was parked up in The White Heart down the road. They could not risk parking in Gordon's yard with all his security staff and cameras. They had changed in every respect and would be unidentifiable as their normal selves. Both were hyper and on edge they had done this sort of thing before but it was almost a primeval state of survival. They had knives and coshes for armed combat but in their hands they carried rifles with silencers and were going to use them.

Danny and peter watched the Transit van pull into the visitors car park. One of Gordon's men pointed to where best park. Jim pulled up and parked. Helped Vera out and removed the painting and waked to the rear door of Mr Gordon's large office area. Danny and Peter watched every movement -just encase. They were admitted to the Welcome room and both sat holding the picture, after the receptionist had made a phone call they entered a small lift and on the third and final floor the lift doors opened and they were transformed into a different world. Every thing was polished and pristine. Onyx, marble, glass wood and brass. Any furniture was antique and immaculate and all around were dozens of Vera's paintings. Thick carpet and chandeliers hung from panelled ceilings. At an oak desk sat Gordon. Slim with sidebalds and a long moustache swept back hair a bit like an old teddy boy. "Vera introduce me Mr Vera ?" he asked. "Not exactly but a very dear friend James Rooney" she replied with a smile. "Please call me Jim" James Rooney offered. "Hello Jim -Jim and Vera" The men shook hands and Vera and Gordon kissed. She unwrapped the painting with jims help and Gordon clapped. "As always Vera its spot on." Gordon handed her a bundle of money and whilst she was counting it he said " If you look down onto the yard your be able to see the new lorry its superb the latest thing in lorries" When she had finished counting and giving Gordon a thumbs up sign they all made their way over to the window looking down into the yard.

As they approached the window a jaguar drove into the visitors car park and parked near by their Transit. van all distracted for a moment they watched two young men step out. Approached by Gordon's security men they opened the boot and handed him a large box. As they looked up and Vera and Jim looked down. Jim and Vera both realised who they were -The Sparrowhawks-at the same moment dull thuds in rapid succession could be heard both Sparrowhawks fell to the floor. The security guard dropped the large box and ran.

Gordon went white. Jim and Vera were speechless'. Then pandemonium broke out. The phone went the bell went. no one dare go into the yard. Gordon refused to phone the Police. Any office staff that were in the building were all in Gordon's office. Some of the security staff were in other parts of the set up, it was one of these that phoned to say he had seen on his security screen two males running off from one of the warehouses. He had checked it out and there was ten or more shells there so it was decided to slowly in a group make there way out.

Gordon told Vera and Jim to go. Saying that he would Handel any trouble and he would let them know how he got on. Besides the blood and mess of violent death they could see the cargo of drugs spelt on the floor near the Sparrowhawks. They looked at the mess and at each other and thought it best just to go. Knowing full well that any drugs that were present would not be by the time the Police arrived. Saying that she would view the new lorry another time they both said it was best that they just leave.

It was in silence that they headed towards the Globe. Did Gordon know that they knew the Sparrowhawks. Did he think they were involved. Both in some guilty dream like state. Both shocked and yet yes both for unexplainable reasons glad that the brothers Nook and Tommy had reached their demise. They returned the van and after visiting Vera's mum made their way by Taxi to the Globe. They had several drinks to help unwind. hand in hand they headed back to Vera's barge. Still light they set off heading for London and the future.

Six months latter they still lived in the barge. They had set up and opened a small but unique art gallery in Argyle Street in the west end. Vera was painting more because they needed more stock. Even at ten thousand pound a picture. The corner shop with Steve was doing well. Jim fell out with sue or more like Sue fell out with Jim. Vera's mum was in a home. She had to be for her own safety. They both saw her every week. Much to Jims delight and Vera's surprise yes Vera was Pregnant.

Goes round comes round.

It was in the papers and on the television. Huge drugs raid on a remote farm area not only netted tons yes tons of drugs but also some hand guns and ammunition. Five had been charged with various drugs charges. It was latter revealed that rifles found at the premises had matched up to the shells found in the Hockcliffe shooting three years previously where two brothers had been killed.

Crushed Orchids had been virtually rebuilt. Vera's barge moored permanently along side it, was used as Vera's studio. She loved working in it and did so most days. Inside crushed orchids clean and tidy with some modern gadgets but was as it had always been. Little Doris was three now. They called her Doris because on the day she was born Vera's mum Doris died. Little Doris was fishing with her Dad. They looked like any other canal side family and in many ways they were. The moneys still in a casket in Barclays Bank.

FINISHED